LOVING THE DUKE

JESSIE CLEVER

SOMEDAY LADY
PUBLISHING, LLC.

LOVING THE DUKE

Published by Someday Lady Publishing, LLC

Copyright © 2024 by Jessica McQuaid

All rights reserved.

No part of this book may be reproduced in any form or by any electronic or mechanical means, including information storage and retrieval systems, without written permission from the author, except for the use of brief quotations in a book review.

This book is a work of fiction. Any references to historical events, real people, or real places are used fictitiously. Other names, characters, places and events are products of the author's imagination, and any resemblances to actual events or places or persons, living or dead, is entirely coincidental.

ISBN-13: 979-8-9881916-5-0

Edited by Judy Roth

For the OG cousin Steve.
Thanks for always making us laugh.

CHAPTER 1

*I*nstead of proposing marriage to the woman he loved, Stephen Marley was hiding in an apple orchard.

To any onlooker, he would appear consumed by his task, diligent even, in his assessment of the trees he had carefully nurtured over the past seven years in the sweeping plain of coastal soil, rich in nutrients from the sea and wind.

But anyone with a keen eye would quickly realize Stephen had conducted the same inspection the previous day whilst also avoiding proposing to the woman he loved.

Dinsmore Castle and the dukedom of Greyfair would be known for their exquisite apple crops, and Stephen Marley would die a bachelor.

He made his way down the row of Sweet Alford until he reached the cross section where they'd planted a row of Backwell Red in experimentation. This type of apple had quickly become their most sought-after crop, and they'd been forced to find another portion of the coastal plain in which to plant. He turned left, heading deeper inland and to the heart of the orchard where if he stood perfectly still, he heard only the sound of the distant sea, the rustle of the apple trees around him, and the beat of his own heart.

He walked quickly, moving deeper into the trees. As the muscles in his right foot tightened with each step, he marveled at how quickly the orchards had grown. What had started as a few trees planted within the sheltering walls of Dinsmore Castle had soon expanded beyond anything he could have imagined.

When he'd first had the idea to increase their apple yield, he had pictured it as another revenue source for the estate, jobs for the villagers and tradesmen. He'd never imagined Dinsmore Castle and the dukedom of Greyfair would become the largest supplier of apples to the nation's cider industry.

He paused briefly, fingering the delicate leaf of a Crimson King, remembering that day when he'd approached his cousin with his idea. Lucas, as usual, had been open to the plan, but he'd had one caveat. He wanted Stephen to take sixty percent of the profits.

Stephen had rejected it, of course. The apple orchards were for the estate, but Lucas insisted. At the time the new railroad spur line had just become operational, and the farmers on the estate were rushing to get their goods to the London markets. Revenue was up, farmers were thriving, which in turn boosted the economy in the village and the need for tradesmen to keep the farms running. Lucas was content to accept forty percent of whatever the orchards brought in.

It came to be that forty percent was a small fortune, and sixty percent fell somewhere between greed and gluttony. Even now Stephen couldn't quite understand what had transpired. He'd been the cast-off relation, the burden to the dukedom of Greyfair, although his uncle and Lucas had never made him feel like a burden. It was simply hard not feel as such when one was sent from one's home because of the unfortunate circumstance of being born with a twisted foot. How could Stephen have not thought of himself as a burden?

Until now.

Stephen's head turned unconsciously to the north. Even from where he stood, he could see the open gable of the cottage, its three dormers standing guard along the prow.

Cottage.

He ran a hand over his face and looked away, a maelstrom of emotions coursing through him. Guilt, shame, unease.

He wasn't yet comfortable in his own newly established role as the orchardist on the estate, and he certainly wasn't used to the salary he brought in. He was suddenly a man of means and…house. He stared through the trees at the dormers as if they mocked him. If he wasn't comfortable with who he was now, how could he possibly expect the woman he loved to be?

He knew perfectly well why he was hiding, and it wasn't because of the thought of proposing. He had already proposed three times, after all. It was because every time he proposed, Ethel Jones gave him another reason for refusing him. And as he gazed at the open gable protruding along the tops of the trees, he wondered if he was headed toward yet another refusal, another excuse, and the worst part was, he really couldn't blame her if she did.

Their courtship had always seemed impossible and yet inevitable at the same time. He could understand her reservations. She was a respected lady's maid while he was the once impoverished and still disowned distant cousin to a duke. What had he to offer her? Any status he held now was made from trade, and while that wasn't as frowned upon as it used to be, it wasn't the same as being born with privilege or earning it through respectable work.

Of course she made excuses. She had her future to worry about. Love could only take a person so far, and in the end, it was money and position that kept a person fed and warm. He had plenty of one and absolutely nothing of the other.

He gripped his crutch with resolve and headed in the direction of the house. He passed several grazing sheep along the way. The animals fed on the undergrowth in the orchards, keeping the trees healthy and prosperous. He was prone to stopping and admiring them at their work, how carefully they moved between rows, eating only what was necessary. But this time he didn't linger.

When he stepped from between the rows of trees, the cottage soared up in front of him. The manifestation of Ethel's last excuse for refusing him—where would they live?

It had been the gamekeeper's cottage in another life of the estate, and Lucas had bidden him use it when they'd come to live at Dinsmore Castle so many years ago. Stephen had never taken his cousin up on the offer, preferring instead the room he'd found tucked under the eaves on the third floor of the newer portion of the castle. It was enough for a single man, and it had suited him well for years, but now...

His room under the eaves was no place for a wife, and it was certainly not a place where he could start a family. He'd approached the gamekeeper's cottage after Ethel's last refusal, intent to see just what sort of work it would need to be habitable again. Only a handful of months ago, it had been overgrown with ivy, shrinking into the forest around it so it seemed like nothing more than the cottage it was purported to be.

Using the wealth he had accumulated over the years from the apple harvests, he had hired a crew to restore it. The damn thing had turned out to be a palace. Once the ivy was removed, the bricks repointed, the shutters repaired, the glass replaced in the windows, and a fresh coat of paint slapped on the front door, the cottage turned out to be a three-story Federal style house with those three proud dormers reaching from its roof. It was breathtaking and beautiful. It radiated with splendor, sending his gut into a spiral.

It was far more than he deserved.

Now he not only avoided proposing again, he avoided moving into the thing. Like everything else about him now, it just didn't feel right.

His eyes dropped to the stone foundation, unease settling in his gut.

He didn't deserve this. No matter that he'd lived his life with the Bennetts since he'd been discarded by his father, Stephen had never quite settled with the family. Despite their love and care, he still felt like an outsider, and now looking at that stone foundation of his cottage, he felt like a farce. For Stephen Marley didn't have a foundation on which to stand. How could he ever think of marrying a woman like Ethel?

This grand house with its fine features and facade. Four whole bedrooms on the second floor without a slanted roof in sight. No cramped quarters here. No ducking under the eaves to retrieve the baby in its crib. No knocking his head against the rafters on his way to bed after a long day in the fields.

This was fine living, and he wondered what Ethel's next excuse would be, unable to fight the feeling she may be right.

"Even if you keep staring at it, it won't get any bigger."

When his cousin Lucas stepped up beside him, Stephen said, "I wager that's not the first time you've said that."

Lucas's expression was nonplussed. "Amelia is looking for you," he said.

Stephen couldn't stop the flinch. Amelia, Lucas's wife, had devised a scheme of exercises she forced Stephen to complete three times a week followed by a torturous administration of salve that left the twisted muscles of his right foot tingling and warm. The worst part about it was the regimen worked. In the three years she'd been forcing him to it, his foot had relaxed in some places and grown stronger in others. There was no cure, of course, but the appendage no longer pained him the way it once had. On his good days, he walked with only a cane, and if he didn't plan on having to traverse the craggy orchards, he chose the cane instead because it gave him greater freedom of movement.

His life had improved dramatically since Amelia had come to Dinsmore, but he wasn't about to tell the Duchess of Greyfair that. He had a curmudgeonly reputation to uphold.

"And you are playing the role of her messenger boy, is that it?"

Lucas looked down, and Stephen's entire body went rigid. Like an involuntary response meant to keep him alive, his body reacted to his cousin in a supernatural way.

"Lucas?" Stephen prodded when his cousin didn't answer immediately.

Finally Lucas raised his head. "No, not Amelia's messenger boy. I've come with a message of my own." He gestured back toward the causeway that led to the castle proper. "I thought it would be best if we spoke here where we're less likely to be overheard."

Stephen's chest tightened. "Why is it that we shouldn't be overheard?"

His cousin was dangerously transparent, and for him to seek subterfuge indicated a serious matter indeed.

But Lucas didn't answer. Instead he reached inside his coat, pulling a folded piece of paper from a pocket there. He extended it to Stephen, turning the paper over in his hand until it caught the light.

Stephen froze. His fingers clenched at his side, his crutch caught between his arm and his torso, unwilling to touch the letter offered him. For it was a letter. He knew that at once when his eyes fell on the familiar wax seal still clinging to the paper even though Lucas had pried it open to read the letter inside.

The seal depicted a shield and cross flanked by a pair of lions. Stephen had thought it too simple of a design for the title it represented, that of the Duke of Norfolk, the cousin to the very Queen of England herself.

Once, when Stephen was still quite young but old enough to have learned from his uncle where he had come from, Stephen had stolen into the library of their home in the middle of the night, not wishing for anyone to see what he was about, not wanting them to discover his weakness, and there he'd pulled down the tome that held all of the insignia of the titles of Great Britain. He'd looked up this very seal, wondering at its parts, wondering if he could ever belong to it.

He swallowed down the memory of the little boy looking for clues of his family in a darkened library and faced his cousin.

"Do you wish to read it, or would you like me to tell you what it says?"

Stephen shook his head. "Just tell me what it says."

Lucas swallowed, pulling back his hand and tucking the offending letter back into the pocket where he'd taken it from. "The duke is coming to Dinsmore. He claims to have heard of our success with the orchards and wishes to see it for himself."

"Lies." Stephen whispered the word in reaction more so than in thought.

Lucas nodded. "I know. The letter is only a guise. Stephen…" But his voice trailed off, so much left unsaid between them.

There was only one reason the Duke of Norfolk would

travel all the way to the coast for a small estate like Dinsmore Castle, and it was a reason for which Stephen did not care. But what he hated more was the sudden surge of hope inside of him, the one he had thought long defeated. The hope that one day his family would come back for him.

Lucas waited a beat before saying, "You must tell her." He patted his coat where the troublesome letter now rested once more inside his pocket. "Before the duke gets here. She'll figure it out then for herself." He waited another beat, licked his lips nervously. "*Everyone* will figure it out."

Stephen stared at his cousin's hand resting against his coat and that damn letter. Everyone *would* figure it out, and yet his jaw remained clenched shut against his secrets.

"When is he coming?" Stephen finally asked after some time.

"Within the fortnight," Lucas said.

Stephen swore softly and looked away, back up at the cottage, which until a few moments ago had been the only obstacle standing between him and the woman he loved.

But now...

"A fortnight doesn't give us much time to prepare. We'll want to have the estate in pristine shape for a visit from the queen's cousin." He was adept at telling his own lies.

Lucas didn't speak, but then he would know not to. Stephen would string together as many words as possible if only to lengthen the distance between him and the truth.

The truth that revealed his greatest weakness. That he still longed for the family that had abandoned him.

Stephen turned and studied the orchards behind him, listened to the birds and the breeze and the sound of his heart thumping in his chest as every possibility thundered through his mind.

He would need to tell her. But how? A glance at the cottage reminded him of just how much stood between them, and he would be forced to add something else. Something they might not overcome.

"Does Amelia know?" He didn't know why he asked the question. It was thinking of Ethel that overwhelmed him, and somehow he thought Amelia knowing the truth would help him.

But Lucas shook his head. "It's not my secret to tell, cousin."

No, it wasn't. Only a handful of people knew the truth, and as the years went on that number dwindled until now there were only three people who knew. Lucas, Stephen, and the Duke of Norfolk.

But when the man arrived at Dinsmore, suddenly everyone would know. It couldn't be helped.

And with this thought came another. What did the Duke of Norfolk desire so badly that he would risk such an exposure of the greatest secret of the dukedom?

Lucas tapped his pocket again. "I'm sure he would have written directly to you, but you know how that would have complicated matters." There was a pause, a heavy one, and then, "If anyone had found out."

His cousin always had a polite way of saying things, and Stephen smiled now. "I know," he said and gestured to the castle. "Tell Amelia I'll be along shortly. I just want to wander through my trees for a bit longer."

Lucas waited, but Stephen didn't say anything more. Finally his cousin reached out and placed a hand on his shoulder.

"You know Norfolk wouldn't be coming here unless it was for good reason."

Stephen met his gaze. "That's the more worrisome part of it."

Lucas's eyes were clear and understanding, and Stephen

knew no matter what, he'd have an ally in his cousin. He always had.

Lucas nodded, squeezed Stephen's shoulder, and turned away, weaving through the trees in the direction of the castle.

Stephen stood there for some time, his fingers working the wood of his crutch absently. Lucas was right. Norfolk couldn't have written Stephen directly with the news of his impending visit.

He couldn't have because Stephen Marley didn't exist.

* * *

Ethel Jones sat very still in front of Mrs. Fairfax's desk.

In her eight years of employment, she'd never been summoned to the housekeeper's office in the bowels of Dinsmore Castle.

Bowels were rather dramatic. Mrs. Fairfax wouldn't have stood for a dungeon for an office. In fact, the room was quite lovely with a fern thriving in a puddle of sunshine from the window and everything.

She was just surprised by the summons. That was all, and she was thinking the worst.

It was what Stephen was always telling her since her mother had gone to live with her sister in the south of France. Ethel preferred to have matters in hand, and when something out of the ordinary arose, it could send her thoughts cartwheeling.

When her mother had decided she would go live with her sister and her French husband, thinking the warmer climate would do her lungs good, Ethel had felt as though her innards were ripped out. It needn't matter that her mother was right. Her lungs had cleared a great deal, and each letter Ethel received was more evidence of her mother's second chance at life.

The last one had even brought news that her mother had taken to making little French cakes she sold at market. She had made a nice cushion of pin money with her sales and was thinking of taking a holiday down to Rome with her sister. Wasn't that lovely?

It was lovely. Ethel could admit as much, but still she felt uneasy with her mother so far away. What if she were to take a turn for the worse? What if Ethel didn't make it in time? What if no one else could take care of her mum like she could?

She realized too late she'd twisted her hands into her apron. Muttering to herself, she smoothed it as best she could, but she'd need to stop by the laundry and iron it before returning to her duties.

It was thinking of Stephen that had done it. She had no business thinking of him during her working hours. He was little more than a terrible, lovely distraction.

Although he never said as much, she knew work had commenced on the gamekeeper's cottage, the one His Grace had given Stephen use of upon their arrival at Dinsmore so many years ago. On an estate such as Dinsmore, it was hard to keep such things a secret, and even if Stephen had never spoken a word of it, she knew it had happened because it was quite literally all everyone had been speaking of for the past several months.

It was a beautiful house set in the orchards, and the staff and villagers were thrilled to see it restored. But the more Ethel heard of it, the more her nervousness grew. Because when the cottage was finished, Stephen would ask her to marry him again, and she was running out of excuses to say no.

When the truth of the matter was, she was simply terrified of marrying him.

Her, a lowly maid on an estate, born of a fisherman and a

seamstress, Ethel wasn't worthy of a man like Stephen Marley. Criminy, he was cousin to a duke after all. Couldn't he see she couldn't possibly marry him?

The only problem with this was the fact that she was utterly and completely in love with the man. Not the kind of love poets waxed melodically about, nor the kind young ladies seemed to gush about in ballrooms.

The kind of love she felt for Stephen Marley was the kind that would last a lifetime. It was built on partnership and compassion and that was the kind of foundation that made love last. She knew it for it was the same kind of love she'd witnessed between her parents.

It made her fear all the stronger when she thought of marrying him.

For what if one day he would realize his mistake? Realize he'd married nothing more than the hired help?

Now was not the time to think of it. Something was amiss at Dinsmore or else Mrs. Fairfax wouldn't have summoned her. Surely her rampant imagination could conjure any number of things with which to plague itself while she waited. Perhaps it was an infestation of termites or worse, bedbugs. Mayhap a plague of influenza had been noted in the village. Or sea monsters had begun to climb out of the ocean, their gnarled hands perfect for ascending the craggy rock face of the castle as the waves of the sea bashed—

She was rattled from her thoughts when the door to Mrs. Fairfax's office opened with a billow of steam and shouting from the nearby kitchen.

"I'm telling ye, Mrs. Fairfax. I'll not have him dragging those hens through here again!"

Mrs. Fairfax turned a calm smile back in the direction of Cook, a single hand raised in acquiescence. "Of course dear, I'll speak to him," she cooed and shut the door, turning a scalding gaze on Ethel. "That woman." Mrs. Fairfax shook her head. "She has a mighty set of lungs, she does."

Ethel smiled softly, unable to summon any more of a response as Mrs. Fairfax made her way to her delicate rosewood desk. Ethel could still remember the monstrosity that had been wedged into this room when they'd first opened Dinsmore. It had been in the old housekeeper's office back at Lagameer Hall, so Ethel was told. Lagameer Hall had burned to the ground in a terrible tragedy, but some things were salvaged, the monstrous desk being one of them.

Thank heavens for Her Grace, the Duchess of Greyfair, who had had the sense to remove the piece of furniture and select a more suitable desk for Mrs. Fairfax.

The housekeeper sat now, placing both hands on her desk momentarily, drawing a very deep breath through her nose as her eyes closed.

Ethel's apprehension grew until her emotions were nothing short of a storm inside her, unable to decipher a single one for what it was. Scared, anxious, overwhelmed, nervous—

When Mrs. Fairfax's eyes fluttered open, Ethel was actively running through a list of nunneries she knew of, especially ones in the south of France. Surely becoming a nun would solve all of her problems.

Mrs. Fairfax smiled. "Oh Ethel, dearie, you look as though you've swallowed your tongue. Is anything amiss?"

Ethel raised her eyebrows. "You've summoned me here, Mrs. Fairfax."

Mrs. Fairfax laughed, the sound light and soothing. "Oh, I'm sorry, child. I didn't mean to upset you. It's only I have some news, and I wanted to tell you first."

"News?" Ethel didn't like news either. News could be good or bad. It could change everything and nothing at all. News was as useful as a hole in one's hat.

Mrs. Fairfax stood and made her way back around her desk, taking the other small chair in the room, the one next to Ethel. She reached over and all but pried Ethel's hands from where she'd entangled them once more in her poor apron.

"Ethel, dearie, it's not so bad as all that. I assure you. Everything is going to work out just fine."

Ethel swallowed. That meant things weren't fine now. But what was it? What had made Mrs. Fairfax summon her?

"Going to work out?" Ethel managed.

Mrs. Fairfax smiled, her round cheeks growing rounder with the expression. "Oh yes, dearie. You see, His Grace has offered me a pension. I'm retiring my position here at Dinsmore Castle at the end of the year." Her smile grew brighter as every piece of Ethel broke apart. "I'm going to Manchester to live with my daughter and look after my darling grandchildren. Isn't that such a blessing?"

No.

No.

No.

None of this was a blessing.

Mrs. Fairfax couldn't leave Dinsmore Castle. Mrs. Fairfax *was* Dinsmore Castle.

Ethel shook her head. "I don't understand. Have we done something wrong?"

Mrs. Fairfax blinked, her eyes questioning until it seemed understanding dawned as she let out a breath. "Oh, my young lady, this is not a punishment. It's time for me to move on is all, and I'm so very lucky His Grace is offering me the chance to do so. It's not every employer who gives their employees such consideration." Mrs. Fairfax shook her head, her steely gray curls unmoving. "No, it most certainly is not."

Suddenly the fog lifted from Ethel's brain, and Mrs. Fairfax's words struck like a pickaxe against rock. Instead of letting the housekeeper hold her hands soothingly, Ethel clung to the woman, her fingers gripping, nearly pulling her forward out of the seat.

Mrs. Fairfax's eyes widened, the dreamy look of only moments before vanishing.

Ethel felt a moment of regret, but her emotions had righted themselves and demanded she act. "What does this mean for Dinsmore, Mrs. Fairfax? A new housekeeper? The staff will be in turmoil."

Mrs. Fairfax tugged a hand free to pat Ethel's gently. "Now, dear, you know no such thing will happen as long as Her Grace is in charge. When has Her Grace ever failed to live up to a challenge?"

Ethel's emotions quieted at the mention of the duchess. Mrs. Fairfax was right. The duchess had proven herself time and again not only in the running of Dinsmore Castle but in the taming of her husband and the raising of three children. Ethel had never met a person more formidable than the duchess.

She loosened her grip on Mrs. Fairfax. "You're right." Ethel pulled one hand free to press her fingers against her forehead. She was surprised to find them trembling. "You're right," she repeated. "Of course you are. Her Grace shall handle this."

When she dropped her hand and met Mrs. Fairfax's gaze again, she was surprised to find her expression clouded once more. Swallowing, Ethel held her emotions in check, waiting for Mrs. Fairfax to speak.

She pursed her lips ever so slightly before saying, "Well, it's that which gave me reason to summon you here today, Ethel."

Dear Lord, she was being sacked.

That could be the only explanation. Mrs. Fairfax was leaving, and Her Grace didn't wish to waste any more time on a nobody like Ethel Jones. That was what was happening. Her heart raced, the sound of her own pulse an echo in her ears, but no—Mrs. Fairfax's expression was something Ethel had never witnessed before. It looked almost like pride.

"Her Grace has asked for my recommendation for a person to fill the position."

Ethel waited, sure there was more, but when Mrs. Fairfax didn't go on, she said, "I see. I'm sure you can find someone among the staff suitable for the position." Her mind filtered through the castle staff, her gaze dropping to her hands as she sorted through the other employees of Dinsmore Castle. "Many of them have been employed at the castle for the duration of His Grace's residency. They would be more than competent in filling the post." Ethel nodded and looked up to find Mrs. Fairfax's brow wrinkled in confusion. "What is it?" Ethel asked.

Mrs. Fairfax shook her head. "Dearie, I've already made my recommendation. I needn't review the staff any longer."

Ethel's shoulders fell, which was ridiculous. It wasn't as if she were fit for the position. She was only a lady's maid and a relatively new one at that. She'd only been in the position for seven years. Some held such a position for near their entire employment before moving into a role as lofty as that of housekeeper. Still, it was a disappointment to hear Mrs. Fairfax had already made a recommendation to the duchess.

Ethel pulled her hands free and smoothed her ruined apron. "I understand." She smiled even though her emotions didn't fit the expression. "I'm sure whoever it is will run Dinsmore Castle with the efficiency the estate deserves."

Mrs. Fairfax smiled in return. "I know she will," she said.

Ethel marveled at the woman's confidence. To know a person so well was a gift. Ethel made to stand. "That's wonderful," she said. "If you'll excuse me, I must return to my duties."

Mrs. Fairfax stood too, a hand reaching for Ethel's arm. "Dearie, don't you wish to know who it is I recommended?"

Ethel shook her head, gathering her skirts to move around the housekeeper in the direction of the door. "As I said, I trust your judgment, Mrs. Fairfax, and I promise to serve under the housekeeper with the same attention and respect I've always given my role."

Mrs. Fairfax's smile was different then, almost dreamy when she said, "I know. That's why I've recommended you for the role."

CHAPTER 2

While he could masterfully procrastinate in proposing again, Stephen could not allow himself to keep his secret any longer, knowing Norfolk's arrival would reveal it anyway. He didn't want Ethel to find out that way, and so after an exhaustive search, he found her in the laundry no less.

The room was empty as it wasn't wash day, and she looked almost lost, hunched over the wooden ironing board the way she was. He stopped in the doorway, just for a second to admire her and think about the oddness of what had happened between them.

It had started off as an easy camaraderie when he'd discovered the diminutive lady's maid could match him wit for wit. It had been a surprise really. She was so small in stature and dedicated to her position. He had almost thought her stuffy when she'd first come to the castle. Then one day, in an all hands meeting about the upcoming plumbing construction to be started at the castle to add much needed modern convenience, Stephen had muttered a ribald comment under his breath. To his amazement, the little lady's maid in front of him had turned her head with a rejoinder, and an odd partnership was immediately formed.

Love came later and was just as much of a surprise. His partner in sarcasm had grown from a lass into a vivacious young woman, and one day instead of trading quips with her, he'd kissed her.

Now as he studied her backside, bent over the ironing board the way she was, he really wished she had accepted his proposal the first time he offered it nearly a year ago. He swallowed, hard, and averted his gaze, scrupulously studying the cold tiles that lined the walls, the empty vats along the side that always reeked of lye.

He had remained a gentleman when it came to Ethel, only taking as much as she was willing to give and even then, exercising caution as she was still a lady's maid and her position relied on her respectability. But God, it was getting harder and harder to take just enough to satiate his thirst for her, and he knew soon he wouldn't be able to stop himself.

Suddenly he wished to propose again. Her excuses be damned.

"Ethel," he said softly with a clearing rattle of his throat.

Her strangled gasp of shock reverberated off the walls of the tiled room, and she sprang back from the ironing board, dropping the pad with which she had been holding the iron.

He came forward, hand raised as if to calm her, but she only swatted at him.

"Stephen Marley, how dare you startle me like that," she hissed, her eyes going to the door as if to ensure her scream hadn't brought anyone running in concern.

As her gaze moved quickly back to him, he thought it likely it hadn't, and he settled his hand on her shoulder. "I apologize, but to be fair, I made a great deal of noise coming down the hall." He lifted the crutch under his arm and his eyebrows at the same time.

Her eyes drifted shut, and she lifted a single hand to her forehead, placing the back of it against her temple. Concern bubbled inside of him, and he swept his hand down her shoulder to her arm until finally he could slip his fingers through hers.

"What is it?" he asked. While he had come to tell her something that could very well obliterate any chance of a future they might have had, the expression on her face had him instantly pushing it aside.

She shook her head and dropped her hand. "It's nothing. What—" She cut off to take a generous sniff. "Do you smell something?"

"The iron is singing your apron," he said.

She jumped away from him, another startled albeit softer gasp springing to her lips along with a delicate curse as she snatched the pad from the floor and pulled the iron from the fabric of her apron, placing it carefully back into the charcoal reserve she had placed on the counter beside the ironing board. This time she pressed both hands to her temples, the pad sagging over her fingers.

"Oh Stephen, it's terrible," she murmured before turning back to him, her eyes huge and worried in her face. "Mrs. Fairfax is taking a retirement. She's going to live with her daughter in Manchester and help with her grandchildren." Ethel shook her head. "Mrs. Fairfax can't leave, Stephen. She *is* Dinsmore Castle."

He stepped forward, finding her hand again and rubbing his thumb over the back of it in small, soothing circles. Her eyes fluttered, but the worry remained.

"While this is shocking and upsetting news, you know Dinsmore will carry on without her. Her Grace wouldn't allow anything else."

She shook her head, sending a wisp of her golden blonde

hair loose, and it fell along her cheek. "That's not the worst part of it."

He couldn't stop himself from reaching up and taking that tendril of hair between thumb and forefinger and tucking it gently behind her ear, his fingers lingering on the smoothness of skin at her cheek before falling away. "What's the worst of it then?"

Ethel bit her lower lip, her eyes wandering his face as if looking for the courage to say whatever she must say. "Mrs. Fairfax has recommended me for the position," she eventually blurted.

Stephen forgot entirely then why he had sought her out. He forgot even where he was, in fact.

"She recommended you for the position of housekeeper?" he asked for clarification.

Ethel nodded, her eyes shining with unshed tears, but Stephen couldn't stop the bark of triumphant laughter that escaped his lips right before he grabbed her. He swept her up, lifting her against his chest, his crutch clattering to the floor and sending a jarring ring through the tiled room, but he didn't care. He kissed the woman he loved, thoroughly and completely as her fingers dug into his shoulders, and her legs squirmed in the air.

"Stephen," she admonished against his mouth. "This is no time to celebrate."

He pulled back just enough to see her face. "Of course it's a time to celebrate, love. You're going to be promoted. I'm so proud of you. You deserve this more than anyone."

Her fingers squeezed his shoulders. "Why are you so bloody encouraging, Stephen Marley? Now is not the time."

He had mercy on her and eased her back to her feet, but he kept one arm around her as he reached up with the other, smoothing the deep line that had appeared between her brows.

"Ethel Jones, you are your own worst enemy," he whispered.

She looked at him warily, her eyes unsure, and he wondered at that. Ethel had grown up in a loving home. Stephen had even had occasion to meet her mother before she emigrated to France. Yet deep within her, Ethel held a fissure where her confidence should have been, and it left wondering at its cause.

"It's not that. I'm simply being realistic." She pressed her hands flat against his chest. Studying the lapels of his jacket, she smoothed them absently. "I'm not a housekeeper, Stephen. I'm hardly a lady's maid." She looked up, and there was worry in her eyes. "And I'm only that because Her Grace has a kind and generous heart."

"Her Grace has a keen eye for talent and a good judge of character. Did Mrs. Fairfax say whether or not Amelia would wish you for the position?"

Ethel bit her lower lip again before saying, "She wishes to have an interview with me about it before the end of the week."

He couldn't stop his smile as he played absently with the loose tendril of her hair. "See what I mean? Amelia knows what she's doing."

Ethel made a scoffing noise and pushed against his chest, but he held her fast. "Knows what she's doing? Mrs. Fairfax said she wishes to know my feelings on the subject." She spoke the word *feelings* as if by doing so she were invoking an ancient curse.

He almost bit his lip this time. "And you think this a bad thing?"

Her expression was one of utter horror. "I don't have *feelings*. I can't afford them."

He let go of her long enough to cup her face in both his hands. "Ethel, darling, you do have feelings. I've seen them.

You're a well of compassion and a sea of patience, and I can't think of a better person to lead the staff of Dinsmore Castle."

She didn't bite her lip then. She merely stared at him, her expression almost resigned. "You'll always support me, won't you, Stephen Marley? No matter how I try to make you stop."

He didn't answer her. He kissed her instead, taking her lips in a long, slow kiss he hoped conveyed the warmth and depth of his love for her. He let the kiss linger, drawing it out until he felt her fingers curling into his chest, gripping the front of his shirt in fistfuls as she tried to hang on to him. Smiling, he released her slowly, languidly, as he eased her back.

Selfishly he watched her coming aware of herself, tugging herself bit by bit out of the kiss. He enjoyed watching her, enjoyed witnessing the effect he had on her, but more, he liked watching her take her pleasure.

Finally her eyes fluttered open, and the worried, frenzied expression that had gripped her features since he'd walked into the laundry dissipated, and she looked more herself.

Until she became too aware, and her eyes widened again, her mouth moving to a soft *oh* as she pushed away from him.

"You're a terrible distraction, Stephen Marley," she muttered as she went back to apron and iron. "I must return to my duties. Her Grace said we're to have a visit from the Duke of Norfolk within the fortnight, and there's much to be done. I can't be caught in the laundry with the likes of you. What will they think of me?"

She had bent over her apron once more and at the mention of the duke, the easiness of kissing Ethel Jones evaporated, and the coldness that had gripped him since his discussion with Lucas in the orchards returned. He bent and retrieved his crutch, taking the time to gather his thoughts.

He had been so focused on finding Ethel and telling her he hadn't quite worked out *how* to tell her. He wondered suddenly if there was a way to word it properly, if there was a special way of conveying his secret that wouldn't mark the immediate end of their relationship.

"Ethel, that's actually why—"

She spun about so quickly he only had a moment to act. Her fingers curled into his shirtfront once more, and he was forced to grip her elbows to keep from toppling them both over.

"Oh Stephen, do you truly think I'm a fit choice for the position?" A deep line appeared between her brows as she scrutinized his face.

He worked to ensure he had the correct, encouraging expression in place instead of the concerned one fueled by his thoughts of the Duke of Norfolk. "You know I do, darling. There's no one more suited to caring for Dinsmore and her people than you. You grew up in the shadow of this castle. This is your home. This is where you were meant to be." He shook his head. "And you've been preparing for this your whole life, have you not?"

The line deepened as she considered his words.

"Wasn't it a scrap of a girl who knocked on those big oak doors of the castle the day we arrived asking for a post?" He couldn't stop the smile from shaping his words. "I've never met someone with such courage as you, Ethel Jones, and you've been proving that since the day I first met you."

With every word he spoke the line between her brows grew fainter and fainter until it disappeared, her face transforming into a tentative smile.

"You really believe that," she whispered.

"I do," he said. "And I also believe your apron is on fire."

She jumped away from him with a squeal of surprise as he went for water, thoughts of the duke and the secrets he would bring forgotten.

* * *

Despite the imminent arrival of the Duke of Norfolk, an estate the size of Dinsmore could not stop everyday business to attend to only the matter of the duke's visit. Other concerns must be seen to in addition to the work required to ready the castle for Norfolk's arrival, and one of those concerns was Mrs. Fairfax's retirement.

Which was why Ethel found herself in yet another interview in only a few days. If Mrs. Fairfax were to retire by the end of the year, her replacement would need to be named within the next few weeks so her training could commence. Norfolk or no, business must continue, the staff must be seen to, and life went on.

Only this time, Ethel kept her hands resolutely on the arms of her chair as she sat before the duchess's escritoire in the library. Instead of assuming a typical office upon her arrival, Her Grace had selected this corner of the library in which to conduct her business. She seemed to favor the room and often exclaimed over the light at this hour.

Ethel didn't notice the light or the books that surrounded her. She could only think about the drumming of her heart and hope she didn't expire before speaking with the duchess.

It was ridiculous really. Stephen was right. She had been a scrap of a girl when she'd come knocking at Dinsmore Castle for a position. She hadn't been scared then. There hadn't been space for such feelings. Her mum was sick, and Ethel needed the funds to care for her. A job at the castle was all there was for it.

But so much had changed since then. For one, Ethel was a proper woman now and quite on her own since her mother had left for France. She'd even taken a room in the servants' quarters now like a proper lady's maid. Everything felt more real than it ever had, and the pressure that accompanied it was at times overwhelming.

How was a mere girl like Ethel Jones supposed to be the housekeeper to a duke's estate?

Because she loved Dinsmore. It was as simple as that. From the wrought iron details of the great oak entrance doors to the delicate etchings of the castle's lady on the iron knobs of the window shutters, she loved every bit of the castle, and she'd be damned if she let anyone else care for her.

She blinked, realizing at some point her heart had slowed. Having been so focused on her own pulse, she didn't hear the door open behind her until the duchess's boots sounded across the wooden floors.

Ethel pushed to her feet, smoothing her new apron and bowing slightly as the duchess came around the seating arrangements to the corner where Ethel waited.

But the duchess being as she was waved off Ethel's bow in the same motion with which she pushed back her dark hair from where it clung to her slightly damp cheeks.

"Oh, no need to stand on ceremony, Jones," she said, sweeping past her to collapse into the chair behind her desk. "I do apologize for my tardiness. Ava thought she saw a sea monster on our walk just now, and Annie was determined to slay it. You know how it is." Through the whole of this retelling, the duchess plucked hairpins from her coiffure and discarded them on the desk in front of her until she could rake her fingers through her hair, untangling the mess it had become likely in her struggles to stop her oldest daughter from slaying a sea monster. "I'm afraid I've ruined all your hard work," Her Grace said, finally looking up, a painful smile on her face.

"I can fix it right now if you'd like. No sense in us just

talking when there's something to be done." Ethel made her way around the desk before the duchess could respond.

Ethel had been Her Grace's lady's maid almost since the time she'd started working at the castle, and there was an easiness between them that came from time and familiarity and from the simple fact that Ethel quite liked the duchess. Everyone did, in fact. Amelia Bennett was a very likable woman, and Ethel was proud to serve under her.

"Don't you require a brush?" The duchess asked, sitting up in her chair so Ethel could reach her long hair.

"Not at all, Your Grace. A simple knot like you prefer doesn't require much." Ethel set to work on the duchess's hair, her fingers moving from memory more than anything else.

"Well then, I suppose we should get started. I should like to know if you desire the position of housekeeper, Jones. I think that's the most important question for me. I know you're qualified for the role, and Mrs. Fairfax is keen to see you replace her, but I'd like to know your feelings on the subject."

Her feelings were she was quite sick to death of everyone discussing feelings. Feelings were a luxury, and she didn't see how they played into something so important as her becoming the new housekeeper of Dinsmore.

Yet her hands had started to shake, and she focused on twisting the duchess's hair into a chignon.

"It's like this, Your Grace," she started, keeping her eyes on the strands of hair, leaning into the familiarity of it. She'd fixed the duchess's hair any number of times in the past seven years for any number of occasions. She knew the feel of it, the way it behaved, the way she needed to place an extra pin along the right side because the duchess tended to thread her fingers through her hair there when she was nervous. "You'd find any number of qualified people to take this post. A person would be right proud to be on staff at an estate like Dinsmore to work for such good people as yourself and the duke. But that's just it. Anyone could fill the role. Anyone, with the proper training could do the job. But that's not enough. Not for a place like Dinsmore."

The duchess was very still beneath her hands as Ethel placed the last pin, securing the chignon and smoothing the flyaways along the crown. She stepped back to survey her work and found the duchess watching her carefully.

"If that's not enough, then what is?" The duchess tilted her head in question.

"Heart," Ethel said, leaning back against the desk and folding her arms across her stomach, nearly forgetting this was a proper interview, and she was being considered for the post of housekeeper. It was easy to forget formality around the duchess. She was so adept at putting people at ease, and Ethel felt the last shred of her nervousness erode away.

"A person can apply for this post with immaculate references and a history of roles that would suit them to the position, but if the person doesn't care for Dinsmore Castle, doesn't have a history with her, the person cannot act on the castle's best interest. Isn't that so?" She straightened and moved around the duchess to the open shutters of the window at her back. Carefully she touched one of the iron knobs of the shutter, outlining the etching of a woman in the metal. She turned back to the duchess, unable to stop her smile. "Remember when you first arrived, Your Grace, and you met our lady for the first time?" Here Ethel tapped the etching of the woman in the iron knob.

The duchess had turned in her chair to watch Ethel, and her eyes took on a dreamy look as she considered Ethel's words.

"I do remember. That was quite a first meeting." The duchess's words vibrated with subdued laughter.

Ethel dropped her hand. "Exactly. You understood our lady straightaway, and you became a part of this castle just as much as I was and Mrs. Fairfax and now precious Annie and Ava." She gestured around her. "You could find someone to ensure the place is dusted, swept, and mopped." She dropped her hands and looked straight at the duchess. "Or you could find someone to care for the lady of our castle." She moved back to the desk and leaned on it with her open palms against the edge, bringing her gaze to the duchess's level. "That's the choice you must make, Your Grace. Do you want someone to manage the cleaning and staff? Or do you want someone who knows how to properly treat a lady?"

The duchess's lips parted, her eyes blinking as she seemed to absorb what Ethel had said, and in the silence, Ethel remembered her nerves, and she wondered at her own audacity. She had an apology ready on her lips when the door to the library burst open without a warning knock.

Mrs. Fairfax scuttled into the room, her cheeks red, her eyes wild. "I'm so sorry, Your Grace, but the Duke of Norfolk has arrived."

The duchess pushed to her feet in a shot. "Norfolk? But we've only just gotten word he was even coming."

"Bloody inconsiderate." The words escaped Ethel's lips before she could stop them, and her hand flew to her mouth as if to catch the curse. She turned wary eyes to the duchess. "I do beg your pardon, Your Grace."

But the duchess only shook her head. "Don't apologize for saying what I was thinking." She made her way around the desk. "Where is the duke now?"

"He's in the courtyard, dearie," Mrs. Fairfax said, following the duchess into the hall.

"Have everyone assemble on the main stairs then. It must do if the duke is going to surprise us like this."

It was customary for the staff of a household to greet

guests on the stairs leading into a house or in front of it, but the duke being in the courtyard already would have made such a greeting uncomfortable and sloppy. The duchess was right to have everyone gather on the stairs in the vestibule.

"Is my husband aware of the duke's arrival?" the duchess asked as they swept into the vestibule itself.

"He's keeping the duke in the courtyard, Your Grace. I believe he's attempting to keep the duke occupied while I fetched you."

The duchess's fingers went to the right side of her head, and Ethel wanted to tug her hand away lest she ruin the newly reconstructed coiffure.

"Do you wish for the children to greet the duke, mum?" Ethel asked. "I can fetch them."

The duchess was already nodding. "Yes, and please gather the upstairs staff. Mrs. Fairfax, I trust you can gather the downstairs staff?"

"Already notified them, dearie," Mrs. Fairfax said. "We'll be assembled in just a moment."

Ethel didn't waste another second. She pulled up her skirts and climbed the double revolution staircase up to the nursery and alerted Nanny to the arrival of the duke while collecting Annie, Ava, and Ash to give Nanny time to right her appearance for Norfolk. She gave Ethel a grateful smile as she ducked into her room off the nursery.

On her way back down, Ethel, with the help of a boisterous and outgoing Annie, alerted the upstairs maids to assemble on the stairs immediately. Ava inquired if they should fetch their tiaras from where they'd left them in the old orchard while they had been playing fairytale princesses. Ethel suggested they save them to show the duke when he was settled. Annie deemed this a fine idea, which had Ava agreeing to it immediately.

Their circuitous route through the upper floors meant

the servants' staircase was more convenient for reaching the assembly on the main stairs, and she ushered the children inside of it and down, carrying Ash on her hip as this stairwell was narrow and descended sharply.

They reached the main floor to discover the sound of hushed conversation coming from the vestibule. The duchess was waiting for them and took Ash from Ethel as she gripped Annie's hand who in turn held Ava's. Ethel became aware of the Duke of Greyfair's voice just seconds before the front door opened, and she stepped into her place above Mrs. Fairfax on the staircase, taking a precious second to smooth her skirts and ensure no hairs had slipped from their pins in her haste to retrieve the children.

But her hand stopped, poised just above her left ear, and she was fairly certain it would stay frozen like that forever.

The Duke of Norfolk stood just inside the door to Dinsmore Castle. He was a tall man but narrow in build. She needn't detail the rest of him though. She needn't have because she knew his face from memory. Knew the feel of his hair between her fingertips, knew the curve of his cheek and line of his jaw, knew the crinkles in the corners of his eyes. She knew every intimate detail of this stranger, and it sent ice traveling through the whole of her body.

Vaguely she understood things were happening. The Duke of Greyfair shuffled nervously back and forth on his feet, a habit so unlike him, Ethel knew he comprehended the delicacy of the situation.

No. The Duke of Greyfair *knew*, and it was a moment in which he understood suddenly everyone would know.

Footsteps.

Pounding, running footsteps.

They penetrated the buzz that had filled her ears, the hammering of her heart, her ragged breathing.

Stephen Marley appeared in the doorway behind the Duke of Norfolk, and it was like seeing double.

Because the Duke of Norfolk was an exact replica of the man Ethel loved.

The worst of it was the way Stephen's eyes found hers as if she were the only person standing there and not one of nearly a hundred servants on display for the great Duke of Norfolk.

He met her eyes only because he knew too. He knew exactly what this moment meant.

Her mind connected the dots, filled in the blanks even as her hand remained frozen above her left ear.

Stephen Marley, the outcast, the unwanted child, the distant cousin who had come to live with his mother's brother and his cousin.

That Stephen Marley was the brother of the Duke of Norfolk. His *twin* brother.

Stephen's hand went up. He reached for her, but she was no longer there.

Pushing past Mrs. Fairfax, Ethel fled.

CHAPTER 3

The stones beneath her feet were slippery, their edges worn into soft depressions by the thousands of feet that had trod on them, and by all accounts, she should have fallen and snapped her neck. But she knew this staircase, had long ago memorized which way it curved and wound down into the darkness beneath the castle.

She had meant what she had said to the duchess—had it been only minutes earlier?—that there was a difference between a person qualified for the role of housekeeper and someone like Ethel who loved the castle.

She'd discovered the secret winding staircase by accident. She'd been going from the old stone chapel, which connected to the castle proper through a narrow stone passageway when she'd tripped, her hand slipping along the fitted stones that comprised its walls. In her attempt to catch herself, her hand had found purchase between two stones, and when she attempted to straighten, her hand pressed farther down instead of bolstering her up. She all but fell into the stairwell then as the stone wall groaned under the weight of her body, sliding back to reveal a landing and the winding stairs.

Stunned, she had stood staring at her discovery for nearly a minute before she collected herself. The wall, she soon realized, was positioned over two iron rails embedded in the floor. It was a simple design and easy to move with even her slender weight. The wedge she had accidentally found between the stones also served as a handle to pull the secret door shut.

She'd never spoken of what she had found and later went back with a lantern to explore. It was to this secret, dark place that she fled now. The space that only belonged to her, so she would be safe from everything but her own thoughts. Except it was her very thoughts that haunted her most.

Stephen was the brother of the Duke of Norfolk. A *twin* brother even. There was no other explanation for it. They were identical. Even she might have mistaken one for the other.

She pressed her hand to her chest the moment she stepped down from the winding stairs. It could have been argued that her racing heart was from the exertion of her flight, but its erratic beat held only one cause.

Her life had just been upended.

Despite her many excuses in refusing Stephen's proposal, she had always felt that one day they would marry. That they could have some kind of life together despite their radically different backgrounds. She could even admit now that when she'd heard she might be selected to replace Mrs. Fairfax, Ethel believed she might be able to convince herself she was worthy of having the cousin of a duke as her husband.

But the *brother* of a duke?

She pressed the back of her hand to her mouth to stop the despair escaping her lips in a feeble cry. She hadn't taken the time to fetch a light, but it didn't matter. She knew the way now, and the little light that came through the sparse windows set high in the walls was enough for her to see by.

She eased along, the floor spongy with moss beneath her feet.

She chose one of the rooms off of the corridor at random, her thoughts too scattered to think any further. She wanted the comfort of the stone to surround her, its coolness to soothe her. It was as though her very thoughts had set her afire, her skin burning with the suddenness of change, and only damp stone could bring her relief.

She held her arms at her sides, her palms open wide as she willed her heart to calm, ordered her thoughts to quiet.

Her first instinct was to rail and accuse. She wished to be angry with Stephen, angry at him for lying to her, for keeping this secret from her. But as cold enveloped her, it cooled her skin along with her thoughts.

Stephen mustn't share any of his secrets with her. A person's past was their own, and she had no right to his. There could be any number of reasons why he hadn't told her. Perhaps he was protecting her. Perhaps he was protecting others like his cousin, the Duke of Greyfair. She couldn't possibly know, and therefore, she had no right to demand an explanation from him.

Still it hurt, that he hadn't confided in her. She had thought...

She shook her head and paced to one end of the small room. No, everything was just as it must be. Stephen was the cousin to a duke and the brother to another, and she was nothing but a lady's maid. There was no future for them. She could continue to make excuse after excuse for refusing Stephen's proposal, making yet another stipulation, another demand, but none of it mattered.

She simply wasn't good enough.

The sound of a boot scraping stone froze her in place for a heartbeat. Her eyes flew to the door of the small room, her ears suddenly prickling.

"Ethel?"

The sound of Stephen's voice drew a muffled groan from her lips, and she shook her head, pressing the back of her hand to her forehead.

She must not have slid the door all the way back into place behind her.

In her haste to be away, she must have been careless. He must have found the door, which meant—

She dropped her hand and called, "I'm down here."

He'd come after her.

This shouldn't have surprised her, but the very idea sent her stomach into somersaults that a man like Stephen Marley should care so for her, care enough to chase after her.

Stephen Marley. Oh God—was that even his name?

She listened to the tap of his crutch on the stone followed by his careful, shuffled gait down the stairs. She didn't move or come out of her small room. He'd find her easily enough.

He appeared in the doorway not moments later, and even by the dim light from the high windows she could make out the roundness of his eyes. But that wasn't all she saw. She saw the sweat along his brow, the pain that tightened the skin at the corners of his eyes, and she wondered if he'd run with his twisted foot. Had his need to find her before she saw the duke, discovered his secret, been so important to him as to cause himself pain?

Her stomach somersaulted again, but then he spoke. "Ethel, is this...a dungeon?"

Her eyes immediately went to the iron manacles that hung ominously from the wall beside her. "I think it is," she said and turned back to study him, to take in his reaction. She enjoyed seeing the world through his eyes. It was a much different view than her own.

His eyes traveled over the cell, at the manacles on the one wall, the broken cot against the other, the small openings tucked close to the ceiling that served as windows but were now so overgrown only a soft light traveled through them.

He gave the iron bars at the front of the cell the longest length of scrutiny before stepping through the door that had come loose from one hinge and nestled one corner into the moss that had spread like a carpet over the floor.

"What is this place?" His voice was less wary as he came toward her, but his eyes still studied everything about him carefully.

"It's where I come to think." She shrugged. "It's quiet. Listen."

He did as she bade him. Silence had always been easy between them. There was no tension to ease with meaningless words, and their bodies were comfortable with each other, unbuffered by conversation.

Soon the space was filled with the rumbling echo of the ocean. It vibrated the stone walls and came up through the soles of her shoes. That was what she loved most about this place. The way the very earth reminded her it was there, comforting her in its consistency and its change at the same time.

"The ocean," Stephen finally breathed, his eyes snapping to hers. "Where are we exactly?"

She gestured to the window high in the wall behind her. "By my estimates, we are on the far side of the original castle. That's why the ocean sounds so close."

Stephen's eyes suddenly narrowed. "How long have you been coming here?"

Even in the dim, she could see the concern in his eyes, and it sparked a warmth in her belly she swiftly dismissed. He had lied to her. She must remember that. But it was so very hard to remember when he looked at her as though he wished to care for her for all the rest of her life.

She was tired enough to let him.

She raised her chin. "Long enough to know I'm not in any danger. Unlike you."

His lips parted as though he had something to say, but he stopped at her pointed words. He looked briefly at the floor before returning his gaze to hers. "I'm sorry, Ethel. That day in the laundry when you set your apron aflame, I had come to tell you then but…" his voice trailed off.

"But I started a small fire in the home of a man who lost his wife in an inferno?" she filled in.

"Something like that," he agreed, scratching the back of his neck. "And I thought I had more time to tell you. Norfolk's letter said he'd be another fortnight. I don't know what I was waiting for. There was just always…"

Again his voice trailed off, but she couldn't fill in the silence for him.

There were just too many things that could have stopped him from telling her, and if she were honest, more than half of them lay at her feet.

"Who are you, Stephen Marley?" she asked, fear beating a funny tattoo in her chest.

He shrugged, the gesture soft and sad. "I'm just me, Ethel. The same Stephen you've always known." He reached above him as if to point to somewhere in the castle where his brother might linger. "I never knew Norfolk. We were separated the moment I was born, and my deformity was discovered."

"You know I don't like that word." Her sudden reaction slowed her heart. Surely if she felt such fierce defensiveness for him when she was angry with him, it said something of her love for him. Perhaps it was strong enough to see them through this.

He let his arm slowly drop. "We were separated, and our mother died giving birth to us. I never knew him, and it was my understanding that our father kept my existence from him." He gave a heartless laugh. "He kept my existence from everyone," he said softly. He moved away from her while he was speaking, and he stood in front of the manacles now, his shoulders slumped. "Lucas's father took me in. He gave me my mother's maiden name to conceal my identity." He glanced over his shoulder at her. "It was a kindness that even now seems impossibly generous." His gaze returned to the manacles. "My father died almost a year ago. I think a part of me has been waiting for this. For Norfolk to show up." Stephen turned to her. "I always thought my father would have left some trail of my existence, and I suppose he did." He gave a shrug. "Or else he told Norfolk before his death."

Something squeezed her chest—sentimentality? Heartache?—she didn't know, but suddenly the strong man she loved looked like a little lost boy to her, and she wanted to go to him, to press herself against him so he would feel he wasn't alone.

Again, his hand went to the back of his neck, hung there as he drew a deep breath. "The cottage is finished, Ethel."

The sudden change in topic left her momentarily baffled. "What?" The word was soft, and he turned to her, his face clear and sure.

"The cottage. It's finished." He stepped toward her, but he was still too far away from her to touch him, to feel his warmth beneath her fingertips. "You said you couldn't imagine where we would live, but I've seen it, and it's more beautiful than I could ever have believed it would be." He took another step, and it was as though he brushed his lips along her neck. The very movement of the air around him sent electricity down her arms, curling her fingers into her skirts. "The bedrooms for our children, I've had them done in pinks and blues and yellows. We'll have one of each, of course, and then the third will surprise us." Another step. "And the orchards come right up to our front door, and the smell of apple blossoms will fill the house in the spring, and the aroma of baked apple pies will keep the house warm when the weather turns cold in the fall." Another step, and she could feel the sting of tears in her eyes. "And our children will play with their cousins in the castle yard, and Annie and Ava will teach them wonderfully dangerous things, and Ash will be forever saving them from certain peril."

The corners of his mouth lifted at this, and unknowingly, her smile matched his, unable to resist its playful pull. He was so close now, she was forced to bend her head back to look up at him. Shadows played over his face, and with the shifting of the light, she saw all the pieces of him. Pieces he hadn't kept from her. Pieces that had been there all along if she'd only known how to see them.

She could picture it, the cottage in the apple orchards, the three children he had so easily conjured, she could see it all, and it was real, and no duke could stop it from happening.

Suddenly she wanted to see it. She wanted to see it so much the air caught in her throat, blocking her words. Excuses had come so readily to her in the past year, but hearing him paint their future so easily, well, it beckoned her.

Her lips parted, but she never got to speak. The sound of footsteps echoed against the stones, and together they turned to the cell door to find the Duke of Greyfair standing on the other side of the iron bars.

"Is this a dungeon?" His voice was an octave higher than Ethel was accustomed to hearing it, and she looked away to hide her smile.

"Yes, it is, cousin," Stephen answered.

By the time she looked back, the duke's eyes were wide in wonder, and he drew a solitary finger down an iron bar as if to test its realness.

"I'll say," he muttered, "I own a dungeon." His finger's progression was interrupted by the cross bar, and it was as though this lifted him from his befuddled stupor. He looked to Stephen. "Norfolk's waiting for you in the library, cousin."

Stephen looked to her briefly, but she knew he wouldn't linger. He wasn't one to tarry when it came to responsibility, and something inside of her fell into place as she watched him leave.

Greyfair stepped into the cell then, his hands to his hips, eyes roaming the room, expression grave. Finally he met her gaze.

"Whatever you do, do not tell my daughters of this. We'll be condemned and sentenced before sundown. The lot of us." He swung his hand around to encompass the entire population of the castle before turning to the cell door, head shaking as he made his way back to the surface.

Ethel couldn't help but smile, the picture of the future Stephen had painted still lingering in her mind.

* * *

HE HAD ALWAYS KNOWN he had a brother somewhere out there in the world, had even known they were twins, but seeing the man for the first time was unsettling.

It was more than just looking into a mirror. It was easy to behold a replica of a thing; it was something else entirely to see that thing move and breathe the same way as him.

For Seward Laurie, the Duke of Norfolk, did indeed move and breathe like him.

Stephen had been in the stable with Barnes, the stable master, inquiring about using their own draft horses to pull the graders along the causeway before the duke arrived when he'd heard the sound of hoofbeats in the courtyard.

Riders came in daily from the rail station or the village with news and deliveries, but there was something different about this sound. For starters, there were several horses, the fall of the hooves against the stones ringing out until the noise was a cacophony against the walls surrounding the castle. This had been followed by the shouts of the stable lads who had been in the paddocks tending the horses. Whoever had arrived was dressed too finely to be from the village or the railroad.

By the time he'd made it into the courtyard, Norfolk had already dismounted. Stephen had known his brother more on instinct than visual confirmation, and he felt sick thinking of the way his body pulled toward his brother. Even as strangers, he knew him, and it sickened him.

Even now he wanted his family to come back for him.

Stephen didn't know how long he stood there, frozen to the flagstones of the courtyard, but it wasn't until Lucas had greeted the man and they had started up the steps of the castle that Stephen realized he needed to find Ethel.

He'd run, even though he'd never been capable of doing so. He pushed his twisted foot, sending pain rioting up his leg, seizing his hip. Still he'd forced his legs to move, to carry him to the woman he loved before it was too late.

But it had been too late.

The image of Ethel's face as it had been in the dungeon moments ago haunted him, and he wondered if he'd already lost her forever.

He studied Norfolk now, taking in the details of him he hadn't had time to consider before.

He had the same brown hair, the same dark eyes, and the same curve to his nose. He had the same lithe build, the same carriage to his shoulders, and the same brackets about his lips.

Except he didn't have a twisted foot.

Stephen clenched his hand about his crutch. "Norfolk."

The duke stood by the dormant fireplace on the opposite side of the room and hadn't noticed him when he'd entered.

He raised his head from where he'd been contemplating the barren grate and met Stephen's eyes. Again, Stephen couldn't help but be unsettled. It was as though he were looking *into* himself.

The duke took a cautious step forward. "Stephen." The word came out slow and unsteady, the two syllables exaggerated as though the duke were worried he'd get it wrong. "Marley, is it?"

Stephen nodded, but he didn't bow or offer a shake of the hand. It was as though an invasive vine had snuck its way into his chest and tangled itself about his lungs. He was afraid to draw a deep breath, worried it might end him. He remained suddenly still, facing this man that was his duplicate and yet a complete stranger.

"I understand Marley was our mother's name before she wed our father." There was a lightness to the duke's voice that Stephen did not possess. He wondered briefly if his own intonations had been influenced by Lucas, who was a much bigger and resounding man than the duke before him. Strange to think the man before him was his brother, similar in so many ways, and yet Stephen was different simply due to his upbringing. Something shifted inside of him at the thought, yet he couldn't linger on it. He needed to keep his wits about him.

"Yes, it was," Stephen replied although he wasn't sure there was a question in there particularly. "What is the reason for your visit?"

The question sparked a flinch in the duke's face, but it was subtle and swiftly repressed. Stephen had no desire for this man to remain at Dinsmore any longer than was necessary, and he wasn't going to tarry while the duke decided to peruse their shared family history.

For it wasn't shared. There was nothing between them except a carefully laid network of lies. For a moment Stephen recalled that night when he'd snuck into the library as a child, and he hated himself suddenly for the weakness. Yet the feeling still lingered. Mostly.

The duke's chin came up ever so slightly as if he were reassessing Stephen. Stephen didn't care. He had nothing to hide from this man, and he certainly had nothing to fear. The Norfolk title had already done the worst to him, and it had saved his life. At least, he thought it had.

"I'd like you to take my place as the Duke of Norfolk."

For a moment Stephen could only stare. He sorted through the duke's words, trying to make sense of them. Finally he shook his head when comprehension remained elusive.

"I'm sorry. Did you just ask me to be a duke?"

Norfolk dropped his gaze, shifting one booted foot and then the other as he placed his hands behind his back and began to pace. Stephen watched him, noting the graceful movements of his brother, the easy way with which he moved his body across the floor. He couldn't stop his mind from wandering. It was impossible not to. He faced the very version of himself he had always wondered about.

The version where he was whole and deserving.

The version where he wasn't a crippled burden.

The version where his family hadn't abandoned him.

He swallowed and closed his eyes, forcing himself to look away. Lucas would berate him for such wayward thoughts. His cousin had never thought of Stephen as a burden. He knew that, and Lucas would be hurt if he knew what Stephen was thinking.

The duke reached the dormant fireplace once more before stopping. It was a moment before he spoke again.

"I don't want to be the Duke of Norfolk." His words were careful, smooth, and spoken with very little feeling. It was as though this were a decision of great calculation he had made some time ago and was now precise in his recitation of it.

"And I don't wish to have a lame foot. It seems we both have things we desire and yet which remain invariably out of our reach."

The duke turned sharply at this, but Stephen did not regret his tone. The thing inside of his chest had grown taut at the duke's words. That this man, this *brother*, who possessed all the things Stephen should have had, should come here to proclaim he wanted none of it was like having the very blood drained from his veins.

But somehow Stephen didn't think he was protecting himself from Norfolk. He felt as though he were protecting all of Dinsmore, this thing he had created with Lucas after the devastation of Lagameer Hall. Dinsmore had been a second chance for his cousin, the man Stephen thought of as his true brother, and in Dinsmore Stephen had found his own path. One he hoped more than anything to convince Ethel to share with him. He didn't want the duke before him threatening that.

He wasn't sure where such strong ideas came from when only days before he had felt so unsteady in his place at Dinsmore. But seeing the personification of his past had his defenses rising.

Norfolk's eyes narrowed, his expression careful now. "Do you remember our father?"

The question caught Stephen off guard. "Of course I don't." He closed his eyes against his own snappish tone, opening them only when he'd drawn a cooling breath. "No, I don't remember our father because I never knew him. I was removed the moment my twisted foot was discovered."

"Removed?" There was something odd about the duke's face, almost as if he cared what Stephen's answer might be.

"I was taken away." There were more words. They were

right there, but his throat had suddenly grown clogged. He swallowed and tried again. "My—" He stopped, realizing for the first time just who stood in front of him, how much this person changed everything. "*Our* uncle—that would be the current Duke of Greyfair's father—later told me I was to be drowned. The doctor who delivered me overheard our father tell a servant to have the deed done, so the doctor took me instead. He kept me until he could make arrangements to get me to Lagameer Hall. That was the previous home of the dukes of Greyfair."

Norfolk nodded. "I know. I went there first looking for you. It was there I learned of this castle." He raised his eyes to glance about the room. "This is quite the operation. I had heard rumors of it, of course, but I must say I'm impressed by the reality of it." He dropped his gaze, and Stephen was struck by the sincerity in his expression. It soon clouded though, and the duke asked, "If you were to be drowned, how did Father know of you?" At this, the duke reached inside his coat and extracted a folded piece of paper. "He left this in his will. It was how I first learned of your existence." He extended the paper to Stephen but checked himself. "Father's words are not kind. You mustn't read this if you don't wish to."

It surprised him, the way the thing that had clawed its way into his chest surged toward that piece of paper. Stephen had never known his father or mother or his twin brother. And now that very brother was handing him the only insight Stephen may ever have to what his father was truly like. Every bit of him, every muscle and sinew, wanted him to reach out and take it, but as soon as the reaction sparked, it died away like a candle blown out.

He shook his head. "I don't need to read it. Our uncle is the only father I wish to know."

The duke waited a beat before replacing the paper in his pocket. "I can respect that."

"As to your question, I cannot say. Perhaps the doctor who saved me informed our father of his actions when I was safely away." He shrugged. "Perhaps we'll never know."

This answer didn't seem to sit well with the duke, but it wasn't for Stephen to make the man comfortable. In fact, he very much desired to make him more uncomfortable, so he asked, "Why don't you wish to be the Duke of Norfolk?"

"I'm going to America."

This was almost as surprising as the duke's request to begin with.

"America?" Stephen repeated the word.

The man nodded and moved away again. Stephen wondered at that. Was his twin brother unable to remain still? There was nothing Stephen enjoyed more than a quiet morning in the apple trees listening to the birds as they started their morning song, content to sit amongst the world and watch it move around him.

"I'm going to start in New York, but I think I'll make my way to that magical place they refer to as the West." He stopped and turned, and for the first time in their encounter, the duke smiled. "I want to be in the thick of it, Stephen. The industry and progress. I want to witness the railroad tracks being laid. The cities they say blossom overnight. The conquering of lands heretofore unseen." His smile then turned from outright enthusiasm to something more precious, like the face of a child on Christmas morn.

It was in that moment the Duke of Norfolk became a person to Stephen. Not the opposition, not his long-lost twin come to upset his life, but a flesh and blood person with his own hopes and dreams. He wasn't that much different than Stephen standing in a dungeon, reciting the dreams he held for his own future to the woman he loved.

And it was in this realization that the Duke of Norfolk became dangerous. Because a person with hopes and dreams was also one who would do anything to achieve them.

"You can't just leave, can you?" Stephen asked the question carefully.

The duke's smile melted like a dying flower. "The cousin of Her Majesty has certain responsibilities that cannot be ignored. If I were to suddenly disappear to America, it would not be treated with a measure of understanding."

A noise in the castle yard drew their attention to the windows beside them, and just through the open gate of the castle walls, Stephen could see the orchards beyond. It was hazy at this distance, not unlike a dream, and the thing in his chest dug deeper.

"I'm sorry, Your Grace, but I cannot assume the title. My place is here at Dinsmore." It was funny how easily those words came from his lips.

Were they true? Did he have a real place here? He'd always been the interloper.

The duke's expression was clouded with confusion. "I'm offering you the chance to be a duke, a duke with close connections to the queen herself, and yet you would refuse such an offer."

"As I said, my place is here." He gestured to the windows. "I helped His Grace build those orchards. It was my idea to implement them, and their operation now consumes a great deal of my time. It would be irresponsible of me to leave."

The duke's gaze lingered on the window. "But they are naught but a cluster of apples. Surely a dukedom is worth more than that."

"Not to me." The edge had returned to his words, and the duke had become an enemy once more.

There was a beat of silence then, taut with the tension that simmered between them.

"You know it would be an easy enough feat." Norfolk gestured between them. "The switch would be effortless to make, and no one would guess you weren't me. Look at us. I thought we might be similar in appearance, but this is rather too good."

Bile rose in Stephen's throat, and he swallowed to keep from being sick. "The answer is still no."

Finally, the duke said, "I find myself at a loss, Stephen." He gave a muffled bark of laughter. "I had thought this endeavor could only be met with success. What man refuses a title?"

"This one." The words came easily.

"Again, I am sorry to hear as much." The duke straightened then, pulling at the sleeves of his coat. "I should like to see the estate while I'm here. The rumors about the rebirth of Dinsmore Castle are spread far and wide across England, and it would be a boon to see it for myself."

Stephen nodded. "I shall fetch His Grace to accompany you on a tour."

"Thank you, Stephen," the duke said. Stephen had almost made it to the door when the duke spoke again. "I hope you realize I know an apple orchard isn't enough to keep a man in a place."

Stephen gripped his crutch more tightly. "Is that so?"

The duke's expression hardened, and the thing inside Stephen's chest burned.

"The only thing that would keep a man from claiming the title of duke is a woman."

Stephen merely turned, giving the duke his back as he left.

CHAPTER 4

She wasn't sure why, but she waited until nightfall to creep out into the orchards.

The castle was silent around her as she made her way down the servants' stairs. She was nearly to the bottom when she thought she heard footsteps behind her. Pausing, she listened, but there was only the heavy quiet of an old stone castle in slumber. She continued down to the kitchen where she fetched a lantern at the rear door before slipping out into the dark.

She could feel the flagstones of the castle yard through her slippers, their hard edges digging into the soles of her feet, and she thought belatedly she should have worn her boots. But the way was so familiar to her, she hadn't thought boots were necessary. How many times had she walked this path with Stephen? Through the castle yard to the gate and beyond to the orchards, wandering through the rows of blossoming trees until at the very heart the old gamekeeper's cottage waited.

She went there now, unable to stay away. The images Stephen had painted for her earlier in the dungeon still lingered in her mind, and she couldn't stop her curiosity from getting the better of her. She must see it.

Perhaps if she saw the rooms he had spoken of she could picture their life there. Maybe it was enough to help her think of Stephen as the man she had fallen in love with and not the secret twin brother of the Duke of Norfolk. It had taken everything in her to follow her heart when it came to the Duke of Greyfair's cousin, and she wasn't sure she had anything left in her to think she may be enough for a cousin to the queen herself.

Holding the lantern high, she threaded her way through the trees. The moon followed her, lighting her path where the lantern could not reach. The trees had grown tall in the past seven years, stretching impossibly toward the sky, their branches heavy with fruit that would soon be harvested. Another successful season awaited the orchards of Dinsmore and its orchardist, the mysterious Stephen Marley.

She swallowed and pushed on.

Approaching from the east, the gamekeeper's cottage appeared at the end of the row of trees, and she could just make out the corner of the house, a neat line of bricks towering up before her. When she finally stepped from the trees, she was practically in the front yard of the house, and she paused, wishing to feel herself a visitor to the place for the first time.

What kind of feelings did this little cottage in the apple trees give her? Was it home? Could it *be* home?

She had meant what she said to Her Grace earlier that day about the castle, about how Ethel loved it in a way no outsider ever could, but the castle had never been home. It was more of a dear friend for whom she felt especially protective. But home? No, never.

Standing before the gamekeeper's cottage, she tried to understand how she felt behind the nervousness that gripped her when things were too big for just her two small hands. She moved carefully around the house toward the front door, taking in the newly repaired shutters that flanked each window with their restored nine over nine panes of glass. It was like something out of a fairytale and in the moonlight, almost seemed magical. But did her future lie inside?

As if prompted by her own thoughts, she reached for the front door before she could stop herself. Stephen hadn't forbidden her from going inside. Besides, it was probably locked tight for the night, the workers having finished their tasks and left the cottage to rest. Except the knob turned easily under her hand, and the door opened with a soft click.

She froze, her eyebrows climbing up as she stared into the darkness of the cottage. Moonlight filtered down like a spotlight on the foyer, and she saw before her the fuzzy outline of a staircase. There must have been a window somewhere above on the landing that let in the moonlight so perfectly, and she couldn't help but feel as though the cottage were calling her inside.

So she went, placing one slippered foot inside after the other. She hadn't bothered with a cloak as the day had been so warm, but the night had proven chilly, and it was even colder inside the cottage. Bracing herself, she stepped fully inside, raising her lantern to take in the place around her.

She could just make out arched doorways on either side of her and a corridor that ran down the length of the stairwell to the back of the cottage. The kitchen would be down there, she knew, and anyone coming in this door would smell the aroma of baking apple pie just as Stephen had said.

Her feet moved as if drawn by Stephen's hypnotic words, and she slipped past the open door, her lantern light bobbing along in front of her until—

The hand came out of nowhere so swiftly her terrified scream was little more than a muffled gasp as it lodged in her throat. The hand was attached to a shadowy, ghostly apparition that appeared in the arched doorway to her left, its menacing shape towering over her as the hand came down to—

Pluck the lantern from her hand.

"I'll say." She meant to truly scream the words, but in her fright, they came out sounding rather whiny.

Stephen glared at her. "I will not trust you in our home with open flame. Not yet."

She had a retort ready on her lips but squashed it when her body tingled at the words *our home*.

She licked her lips and said, "Hello," quietly instead.

His smile was slow, almost tentative, and she hated how much things had changed between them in the course of a single afternoon.

"Hello."

She expected him to say more, but he didn't, and silence hung between them. It was an easy silence. It usually was as neither of them felt the need to fill spaces with unnecessary words. She could stand there forever, studying his face in the changing light of the lantern, but instead she gestured to the house around her.

"I wanted to see it." She didn't know why she was whispering, but suddenly there was a gravity to the situation she thought words might break.

"So you decided to sneak in in the middle of the night?" There was no accusation in his voice even though she deserved it.

She pressed her palms against her thighs and looked down at her hands. "I thought you might be occupied with His Grace." She needn't specify which one, and when she looked up, she found his eyes had grown dark even in the lamplight.

"I'm finished with the duke." Again, his tone held no accusation, but his words held any number of meanings, which left her more confused than when she'd first discovered his secret.

Again, he said nothing else, and she realized she had no right to the business between a duke and his brother. The very idea someone as lowly as Ethel Jones being privy to such information was ridiculous, and she felt the crush of the afternoon on her shoulders.

She moved toward the still open door. "Right, I'll just be—"

"He asked me to take his place as the Duke of Norfolk."

"Cheese and crust." She pressed her hand to her mouth, shocked by her own profanity.

His smile was a little surer now. "That's not quite what I said."

She let her hand fall away from her mouth. "What did you say?"

"I said I wasn't interested."

Was that her own beating heart or was there a battalion of squirrels executing drills upon the roof?

"You're not?"

He shook his head slowly, his eyes never leaving hers. "Of course not. Everything I want is right here."

Did he mean her or this cottage? Oh God, someone had scrambled her brains.

"It is?"

Now the silence was heavy between them, thick with unspoken words and swirling emotions, but she couldn't bear to prompt him. His answer had to be his alone.

But he didn't answer. Instead he straightened and offered her the elbow of the arm that held his crutch. "Miss Jones, would you like a tour?"

The question should have been a simple one, but there was a weight to his words that kept her from answering. He wasn't just offering to show her about the cottage. He was asking her to see the life he had imagined for them. The life she very much wanted.

There were a thousand things she wished to ask him about his encounter with his twin brother. How had it felt to finally meet him? Had Stephen longed to meet his brother his whole life or had he always harbored resentment for the duke? She didn't know. Stephen had never spoken once of the family that had abandoned him, and she had believed it to be a subject that held very little interest to him.

But was that true?

She studied his face, so familiar and yet now so strange, and she wondered what, if anything, was true between them. Was she letting the truth of his past ruin everything they had? Was it warranted? Stephen had been cast out as a baby, not even hours old. What role had he to play in all of this besides concealing the true identity of his birth family?

Quite frankly, if it were her, she'd have done the same thing. The Norfolk title was a weighty one. Who would wish to live under its pressure?

She slipped her arm through his. "A tour is just what I had in mind."

Something passed over his eyes then, and she felt a flicker of guilt that it might have been relief.

He turned them about, lifting the lantern above them. "This, Miss Jones, is the parlor," he began.

He drew her through the cottage, pointing out each detail of every room from the wide, plank oak floors with their new coat of stain to the Danish wainscot oak paneling in the dining room. The kitchen was outfitted with not only an iron range but a water boiler and a sham for the kettle. They circled back around to the opposite side of the main staircase to the family sitting room.

She stopped in the door, unable to move farther as she

stared at the opposite wall. Although it had been the gamekeeper's cottage, she was coming to understand some architectural design had gone into the building of the place, and at times, there were thoughtful touches added to each room.

In the sitting room, it was the fireplace. It wasn't the structure itself so much although it was a gorgeous inglenook fireplace with a recess made of deep red brick and decorated with iron details of vines in bloom. It was the fact that when she saw that fireplace, she could picture herself sitting in front of it, Stephen at her side while he read the day's news to her as she darned their children's socks.

One of each and a third one as a surprise.

Stephen was saying something about the coats of paint and the plastering work the room had required, but she heard none of it. She could only stare at the fireplace and see the life Stephen had started to shape for them, the one he had conjured with his words first and now the one she saw for herself in the home he had prepared for them.

She glanced up at him as he pointed out the new woodwork framing the doorway, and she wondered absently if he were an earl or a marquess or something. It was common for younger brothers of dukes to hold a courtesy title. But somehow she couldn't quite think of the man beside her as any of those things.

He was only Stephen.

Her Stephen. The man she had fallen in love with.

"You're staring." His whispered words shook her as though he had shouted them, and she started, tugging on his arm as she pulled herself from her thoughts.

"I was just thinking," she said, struggling to make some sense of what had become of the life she had thought so ordered only hours before.

"Well, before you come to a conclusion, there's one more thing I wish for you to see."

He beckoned for her to follow him up the stairs. She wanted to make him stop, to ask him all the questions rampaging through her mind, but curiosity as always got the best of her, and she picked up her skirts, letting her hand trail over the smooth banister as she made her way to the upper floor.

The landing turned into a small hallway that ran to the front of the house, and four doors opened off of it. He led her to the farthest one and disappeared inside. She ducked her head around the corner, not quite sure what to expect when she saw—

A bed.

The cottage was sparsely furnished as though some furniture had been left behind, and the builders had worked around it. To see a bed neatly assembled complete with a mattress and hangings was startling.

But then Stephen spoke as if reading her mind. "I wanted to make sure you woke every morning with the best view from the house. I needed the bed to get the angle right."

She glanced at him, but her eyes were drawn back to the bed. The room was larger than she had expected, and she wondered if the gamekeeper had once slept here. On the other side of the bed, there was a single chair in front of a small fireplace, but otherwise the room was empty, much like the rest of the cottage.

Tentatively she stepped inside, and only once she was standing next to Stephen again did she recall his words.

"Best view from the house?"

He simply gestured to the row of windows at their backs. She turned and—

Stopped.

It was the castle bathed in moonlight and shrouded by passing clouds. The darkness of the ocean fell around it like a cape, comforting its lady even in the darkness.

She shivered, her words unsteady. "Oh, Stephen."

He shifted beside her, the sound of his crutch scrapping wood as he set it and the lantern aside to kneel before the fireplace. "You're cold," he said, mistaking her rapture for something else entirely as he began to lay a fire in the hearth.

Absently she was aware of him behind her, the sound of kindling snapping, the strike of a match, but her eyes could only take in her castle through the window.

He had gotten it just right. From where the bed was situated she would see the sun rise over her castle every morning for the rest of her life.

She turned about so quickly her skirts brushed the wall at her back. "Have you told His Grace—that is Greyfair—of what the duke asked of you?"

He looked up from where he was nursing the fire, his eyes serious. "The only person I wanted to tell was you."

"Me?" It was all she could do to manage the word. She swallowed and summoned her courage. "Then why are you hiding out here in the middle of the night? Why didn't you come to me?"

He drew a breath then, a heavy one, and she felt that same flicker of guilt. He got to his feet, brushing his hands against the thighs of his pants as he moved to stand in front of her.

She wanted him to touch her suddenly, but he didn't. He stood perfectly still, a calculated space between them.

"Because I know I upset you," he said. "And I know you prefer to have some latitude to think when things go unexpectedly. I've learned as much after three rejections of my proposal."

"I didn't reject you." She spoke the words so quickly it was like tossing water on a fire she hadn't meant to start and was desperate to put out. And then the next words came just as easily. "Stephen, I very much want to marry you." She took a step forward, closing the gap between them, and pulled his hands into hers. Looking directly into his eyes, she said, "Ask me again. Right now."

He blinked, shock evident on his face as he said, "Ethel Jones, will you—"

"Yes!" And then she threw her arms around his neck and kissed him.

* * *

IT WAS LIKE AN EXPLOSION.

She'd been kissing this man for more than a year. His lips were as familiar to her as her own, but just then it was as though she were kissing him for the first time. There was a newness to it, like a light had been thrown into an old and cramped room until all the shadows were disbanded.

She couldn't think of him as the Duke of Norfolk's brother. She could hardly think of him as Stephen. The kiss shattered any coherent thought she might have had, and instead her body was filled with only touch, taste, and sound. The way his beard scraped along the sensitive skin of her neck as he moved his lips over her jaw and lower, her head tipping greedily back. The way her skirts rustled as his hands clenched the fabric at her back as he dipped her into his arms. The sound of the fire crackling competing with her own ragged breath.

"Say it again," he whispered against her ear before he sucked her earlobe between his lips, his teeth grating deliciously against her skin.

"Ah," was the only sound she managed, and then it was more a strangled moan than an actual word.

"Say it," he persisted, his voice guttural in her ear.

She pulled out of his arms and pressed her hands to his chest to hold him at bay. She wanted to look at him when she said the words. She wanted to see his eyes, watch how they darkened, watch his lips part just the slightest of degrees, watch his breathing hitch.

"I want to marry you, Stephen Marley," she said. "Just as soon as possible."

His eyes did change. They darkened, impossibly so, but the rest of him remained so still she wasn't sure he heard her. He watched her with those hungry eyes as if she were prey, and something deep inside of her sparked to life, a fire burning low in her belly.

He had never looked at her like that before, like he wished to devour her. She should have backed away, fled for safety, but instead she stepped forward, lifted her face to his, beckoned his kiss.

And he took.

He took her, all of her.

She wasn't sure who first moved toward the bed, but soon they tumbled upon it, and she was pinned beneath him, his weight pressing her into the bare mattress at her back.

Intimacy between them had always been so tame, but there was nothing tame about the way his hand tugged at her skirt, lifting it inch by hurried inch as his teeth bit small kisses along her jaw, down the line of her neck, and lower until she arched into him, unable to hold herself back.

He groaned somewhere around her collarbone, but by then his wandering hand had discovered her ankle and then her calf, and the fire he'd started inside of her with only his gaze burst into an inferno, and she clawed at his back, wrapping her other leg about him as best she could even when her skirts got in the way.

It fluttered briefly through her mind that what was happening to her shouldn't be happening at all. That this incredible, beautiful man loved her, wanted her for his wife, was taking her as his. That she *wanted* him to take her. That she wanted all of him just as he wanted all of her.

That was until he sat up and rolled away from her.

She blinked into the shadowy darkness above her, noting the brown of the rafters that crisscrossed the ceiling. Finally she turned her head against the mattress to find Stephen sitting fully upright against the headboard, his chest heaving. He laid an arm over his eyes and let his head fall back against the wall.

Rolling, she made her way to all fours, crawling across the mattress toward him. She'd only made it a few inches when he threw out the arm that had been over his eyes, saying, "Stop."

She did as he said, rendered motionless more by the pain in his voice than by the word itself. She shifted, sitting back on her haunches, her hands folded primly in her lap even though her body radiated a fire that would only be satisfied by the very man who now seemed so resolute in his desire to not touch her.

"Stephen," she tried. "Are you doubting my wish to marry you? Because I—"

He waved that hand at her. "It's not that."

"Then what is it?" She dared do little more than whisper the question. A sudden fear that he'd changed his mind seized her. She looked down at herself, noting the apron still pinned to her dress and the small dot of shoe polish she'd been unable to get out of it. "Is it my uniform?" she asked. "Because I can take it off." She moved to unpin her apron, but this only caused him to sit up in a flash, both hands waving wildly in protest.

"No." The word shot from him like a ball from a cannon. "No," he said more quietly. "Please do not remove your clothing. That will not help at all. It's—" He dropped both of his hands as if all the air had left him, and he slouched back against the headboard. "Ethel," he said, scrubbing one hand over his face.

She inched forward the smallest of degrees, placing one hand tentatively on his knee where she felt it safest. She just wished to touch him even if he seemed to have changed his mind about taking her.

Once more he sat up so quickly it caused a gasp to lodge in her throat, but then he captured her face in the cradle of his hands so gently, so exquisitely, it brought tears to her eyes.

"Ethel." He spoke her name more reverently than a prayer. "I want you more than a thousand desires. I need you more than the air I breathe. But I won't steal you like a thief in the night." He moved his hand, stroking her cheek with a single finger. "I've waited so long. I can wait a little longer. I respect you too much not to. I want this bed to be our marriage bed in the home where we raise our family. I won't accept anything less."

Marriage bed.

She stared into his beautiful eyes. "I think I enjoyed what you just said better than all the times you've told me you love me."

The trepidation in his eyes melted away at her words, and a smile slowly crept to his lips.

"Then will you forgive me for not finishing what I foolishly began?"

She gripped his wrists. "Only if you promise me we'll finish this on our wedding night."

His smile grew, and he even dared to lean toward her. "That is a promise I can keep."

He kissed her softly, tenderly, and the rest of the world fell away. There was only the touch of his lips against hers, the beat of his pulse under her fingertips, and the yearning she felt in her heart for this man.

He pulled away all too quickly and slumped back against the headboard, a look of despairing defeat on his face. She tugged her skirts from under her knees and crawled over to him, dropping onto the bed beside him. She was careful to keep the tiniest of space between them, their shoulders never quite touching as she leaned back against the headboard.

"You know," she began. "You're ten times the man Norfolk is. I don't care if he is a duke. That's only a circumstance of birth." She turned to take in his face. "He had nothing to do with that."

Something passed over his face then, but it might have only been a shadow. He gave her a tired smile, and she knew it was time to speak of happier things.

"It is a lovely view," she whispered, taking in the night sky that had turned a shade of blue gray only found right before the dawn. Reaching out, she took his hand into hers and drew it onto her lap. "Watch the sunrise with me," she said, and this time his smile held a little more sign of life. She squeezed his hand. "Tell me about growing up with the Duke of Greyfair."

Stephen barked a laugh. "Lucas?" He shook his head, jostling the headboard against the wall behind him. "It was mostly giving him ample opportunity to call me a dunderhead."

She laughed too. "Did you deserve it?"

He turned his head toward her. "Probably." He thought a beat. "Mostly." He thought some more. "Likely every time."

Her laughter came more easily now, and she smiled, drinking in the sight of the man she loved sitting next to her, holding her hand. "And did he never make a mistake?"

His face took on a faraway look then, and for a moment she thought she might have lost him to his memories, but then he said, "I think he just never got caught." His smile was wistful and tinged with sadness as if mourning for his long-ago childhood. He met her gaze. "Lucas is five years older than I am. It was just the right difference in age for him to show me how to do things and perhaps for me to do them better than he, but I never did want to do them. The important part, the part that mattered, was the showing."

She threaded her fingers through his, trying to understand what he meant, but as she had no siblings, she couldn't quite understand what it was that transpired between them, but she knew whatever it was, was special and dear.

"You're so lucky to have grown up with someone like His Grace." She turned over his hand in hers and traced the lines of his palm. "To have someone know you like a brother."

He was quiet, and when she looked up, she saw an odd expression on his face, one she couldn't quite name, but then his gaze shifted to the window and the light that had grown bright there.

She set her gaze on the distant castle just as the first of the morning sun broke over the hills, sending its light across the orchard to the castle beyond.

They sat there, together, watching the sunrise, cocooned in the comfort of silence.

CHAPTER 5

The sun had almost risen when Stephen reached the edge of the cliff.

The view from there was much different than it had been when they'd first come to Dinsmore. For one thing, there was a beast of an iron railroad cutting through the valley now that was the lifeblood of the village and the estate farms. It was the very reason Dinsmore was able to operate a flourishing apple business. It was everything Lucas had fought for when he'd first come to the castle.

And it was nothing to Stephen.

None of this belonged to Stephen. It belonged to Lucas, and sitting there on his horse, gazing down at the valley, he was reminded again of just how much *wasn't* his.

He should be happy. Of all the days of his life thus far, this should have been his happiest, and yet it wasn't.

The woman he loved had finally agreed to marry him. He'd snuck her back into the castle—or rather she snuck herself—through a smuggler's tunnel that opened in the original orchard inside the castle walls and connected with the dungeon he had only learned was her retreat the day before.

He'd been right in selecting the eastern bedroom as their own. The castle was precious to her as he'd known all along, and to have it be the first thing she saw upon waking for all the rest of her days seemed the only thing that was right.

And yet, even now he found himself on the ridge overlooking the valley, his own retreat when things worried him too much.

He wasn't surprised when the sound of hoofbeats reached him through the forest at his back. He hadn't been the first person to make this cliffside his retreat, and in seconds, Lucas appeared beside him, his horse puffing from the exertion of climbing the ridge.

"You didn't sleep in the castle last night," Lucas said by way of greeting. "Do you not wish to be under the same roof as Norfolk?"

Stephen gave a snort. "Hardly. The man concerns me about as much as a fly on a horse's rump would concern the horse." He turned his head and met his cousin's gaze. "It's what he might do to the people I love that concerns me."

Lucas adjusted in the saddle. "Has he made any overtures to cause such concern?"

"He wishes for me to take his place as the Duke of Norfolk."

Even in the early morning buzz of a world awakening, Stephen heard Lucas's quick intake of breath.

"Hell's teeth," his cousin muttered. "He can't be serious."

"I think he is," Stephen said, turning his gaze back to the valley below them. "He said something when I refused him."

"What was it?"

Stephen shook his head slowly, replaying the encounter with his twin brother from only the day before, trying to make sense of the strange meeting. "Norfolk wasn't happy when I refused him. He seemed to think a man wouldn't choose the life I lead over his." He threaded the reins through his hands, feeling the leather tug against his gloves. "He said only a woman could make a man refuse a dukedom."

Lucas straightened beside him. "Do you think he'll try to do something to Ethel?"

Stephen couldn't even contemplate it. Thinking Norfolk might harm Ethel in some way had his chest squeezing and his breath freezing in his lungs.

So instead he said, "She's finally agreed to marry me."

Lucas's smile was slow and full, the smile of a man who had discovered deep and profound happiness in his own marriage. Stephen knew because he witnessed it every day. Even when Lucas's daughters forced him to walk the plank or play debutante ball. Lucas was usually forced to play the role of visiting princess from a small European principality. He wore a tiara well.

Lucas's smile was swift to dim though. "And yet you're visiting the cliff this morning? Do Norfolk's words trouble you so?"

Stephen shifted. "I'm not sure what is more concerning, Norfolk's blatant request or his quiet observations."

"Did he give a reason for wishing to forfeit his title?"

"The man desires adventure, and like so many men before him, is willing to give up everything for it." Stephen met Lucas's gaze. "He says he's going to America."

Lucas swept a hand in front of him, gesturing to the still new railroad cradled in its depths. "Is there not enough adventure here? The rapid growth of industry is enough to scramble the mind. Surely it's enough for him."

"I think it is exploration that compels him. He mentioned going west once arriving on the continent."

Lucas grimaced and looked away. "Red rock and desert

sands," he mumbled before looking back at Stephen. "Not the life I wish to lead."

"Me either," Stephen agreed.

There was a space of silence then as each man took in the rolling valley, the gentle sweep of forest into meadow and the ultimate drop of the ridge. The horses shifted beneath them, their soft snuffs of adjustment blending with the call of birdsong.

"Cousin," Lucas finally said, his voice rippling with caution that had Stephen sitting up in his saddle. "What kind of life is it you do wish to lead?"

Stephen looked sharply at his cousin. "The one I'm living now. Why would you even question it?"

Lucas's brow furrowed, and he shook his head only slightly as he said, "You always seem to be looking for something. I thought for a long time it was about Miss Jones, but even now, I can feel this restless energy about you. What is it, cousin?"

Stephen could only stare. "Why do you think I'm restless? You know Dinsmore is my home as much as it is yours."

"Is it?"

Such a simple question and yet it had the power to cut to the bone.

Stephen looked away, following the swoop of a sparrow from the forest to the meadow, along the edge of the ridge. He let his thoughts tumble with the sparrow, and when he finally spoke, it wasn't what he thought he meant to say.

"What was it like for you when I arrived at Lagameer Hall?" He looked back at Lucas to catch his reaction to the question, but his cousin's expression remained unchanged. "I mean," he went on, feeling nerves suddenly constrict his throat. "You were a boy of five by the time I came to live at the Hall. You had a whole life by then, a family, and your place in it. Then I came in and destroyed all of that."

Stephen started when Lucas's hand landed on his arm, his grip tight.

"Don't say that," Lucas said, his voice suddenly as tight as his grip. "You didn't destroy anything. Do you have any idea how I longed for a little brother?"

This surprised Stephen, so much so that his horse shifted beneath him as if feeling its rider's shock.

"Little brother?"

Lucas released his grip on Stephen's arm. "The only thing I was upset by was the fact that you were so tiny. How could I race you to the top of a tree when you couldn't even roll over?" Lucas's voice had remained tight, and it was a moment before Stephen realized he joked.

"I'm sorry I disappointed you," Stephen murmured.

Lucas stared at him. "I've been waiting for that apology for more than twenty-five years."

Stephen laughed, and he found the sound broke something inside of him that had been holding him back.

"I don't have anything, Lucas. Not really. I don't have roots like you. I don't have a family. I'm grateful for your father and what he did to protect me, and I'll never be able to tell you how much you mean to me, Lucas." He couldn't hold his cousin's gaze any longer, so he looked away as he took in the bigness of the world around them. "But I've always felt there was something I was missing. Something I lost or maybe never had in the first place." He looked back at Lucas. "I don't know how to build a life with Ethel on something that isn't there."

Lucas's expression had grown more concerned as Stephen talked, and now it held a degree of confusion. "From what do you think this feeling of incompletion stems?"

In an instant Stephen was back in the library at Lagameer Hall, scouring a book that weighed more than him for answers to who his family was. He knew what it was that plagued him, but somehow it felt disloyal to speak the words to the cousin who had accepted him as family since the moment he'd come into his life.

But this was Lucas, and Stephen knew he would listen before all else. So he finally spoke the thing that had crawled into his chest so long ago and had grown tentacles he feared he'd never be able to sever.

"I don't know who I am, Lucas," Stephen finally said, the words almost stuttering as he forced them out. "I know nothing of the family from which I was birthed, what they were like, whether or not I look like my mother's father or my father's father or if I like marmalade on my toast like my great aunt Gertrude. I don't even know if I *have* a great aunt Gertrude." He shook his head, the words drying up. "How can I know who I am if I don't know where I've been?"

For just a second, Lucas's expression changed to surprise, but it was there and gone so quickly Stephen couldn't be sure he'd even seen it.

"And Norfolk's arrival hasn't provided you with any clues as to who you are?"

Stephen couldn't help but think of the first moment he'd seen his twin brother. The way his mannerisms and the way he moved were more upsetting than his resemblance to Stephen had been.

He swallowed and shook his head. "I don't think Norfolk has any more information than I do."

"How is that?"

Stephen hated the words that bubbled to the surface then, the ones he'd been unable to shape for so long because he couldn't quite believe they were the ones to which he required an answer. "I think I need to understand why they gave me away. I was their son."

Lucas's eyes widened. "Then you seek answers from the

dead." The shake of his head was heavy with sorrow. "I'm afraid that's a resolution you may never get."

Stephen nodded, pulling the reins through his gloved hands just to feel the tug of the leather. "I know. That's the worst of it." For a moment he could picture the whole of his life stretched out before him, his greatest question going unanswered.

"Is there another way for you to figure this out, cousin? It would be a shame if your past kept your future from happening."

Lucas's words upset something inside of him, and in an instant he thought of Ethel, of their impending marriage. What if his misgivings stopped it all from happening? What if he couldn't bring himself to go through with it?

What if not knowing who he was prevented him from becoming who he was meant to be?

Ethel's husband and a father to their children.

The future was suddenly dismal when it should have been the brightest it had ever been.

Was there another way to discover the answers he sought? He couldn't think of one, but then he'd always done his best thinking in apple orchards. He adjusted in the saddle, squeezing the sides of his horse until it began to move, turning about in the direction of Dinsmore.

"I think you might be right, cousin," he said. "I think I shall look for a different route to my past."

Again he thought he caught that curious expression on Lucas's face, but again it was so quick it might have been a mirage.

Lucas's voice was soft with sincerity when he said, "And I shall hope that you find it."

With that, they rode back through the forest to Dinsmore Castle in silence.

* * *

WHEN SHE JABBED herself with the needle for what felt like the hundredth time, Ethel set the gown aside and took a deep breath through her nose.

She'd been trying to fix the hem on the duchess's ballgown for the better part of an hour now and had accomplished little more than making herself bleed through a countless number of pinpricks.

She was not merely distracted. Her head had clearly detached and left itself in their cozy little cottage at the edge of the apple orchard. The night spent in Stephen's arms had been too short, but he had been right about the view. When the sun had crested the horizon, it had bathed her castle in an orange glow, setting it afire like the gem it was.

She could gaze upon that view all the mornings of the rest of her life.

And she would now. She'd agreed to marry Stephen. Finally. And somehow the world hadn't ended. Everything was just as it should have been. She went right back to her duties in the castle that morning, attending to the duchess's toilette and starting on her day of repairing Her Grace's wardrobe and laundering the gown she'd worn to Ava's first riding lesson, which had resulted in a muddy catastrophe.

Yet she was still betrothed to the duke's cousin.

The Duke of Norfolk's twin brother.

She stilled, her thoughts arrested by that single one. Yet it didn't hold the power it had the day before, and she wondered if over time it would weaken more and more until soon it would hold no sting at all.

Stephen would be her husband soon. Her *husband*. Surely that held more power than anything.

She pushed to her feet, leaving the ballgown in the dressing room. The gown which had played the role of victim in the riding lesson incident had required a full washing and while it wasn't wash day, the gown simply couldn't wait. As soon as she'd finished with the duchess's toilette, she'd set to work on it. It had been soaking in a vat of lye for several hours now, and she wanted to check on its progress.

Besides, the walk down to the laundry might help to clear her head.

The castle was quiet this time of day as the duke and duchess were mostly outdoors or in the village attending to estate business. The children were in the nursery with Nanny, and as it was time for lessons, it was even quieter than normal.

Ethel made her way into the corridor and toward the rear of the castle where the servants' staircase would take her down to the laundry. The family's rooms were in the newer part of the structure, and she would be required to wind her way around the double revolution staircase to the original structure and the cramped staircase that led all the way to the basement.

She had just passed the double revolution staircase when she felt as though she were being watched. This wasn't the first time she had felt as much in the castle, and for a few seconds, she simply ignored it. The old place was full to the brim with ghosts, but they'd never haunted her. It was merely like feeling the echo of a warm presence around her, and she'd always welcomed the company. But this wasn't the same feeling, and her steps slowed on the carpet until finally she was forced to turn around.

Her smile was automatic, more like a reflex than actual thought when she saw a face she knew better than her own. Until her eyes fell upon the clothes the gentleman wore, and she realized at whom she was really looking.

Her smile vanished, and she dipped her head in the

acknowledgment protocol required. "Your Grace," she murmured. "Is there something I may assist you with?"

The Duke of Norfolk slinked toward her like a feral cat, all sinewy muscle and long, exaggerated strides as though hunting prey. How could she have mistaken this man for Stephen even for a second? He moved entirely differently, he breathed entirely differently, he even smelled different. He smelled of sandalwood and bergamot, manufactured scents that could never compare to the fresh ocean air and apples she associated with Stephen.

Norfolk's smile was as slow and calculated as his stride. "You're the duchess's lady's maid, are you not? Jones. Do I have that right?"

There was no reason whatsoever for this man to know her name, and her defenses immediately rose. She squared her shoulders and lifted her chin.

"The name is Ethel Jones, Your Grace. I've been a lady's maid here at the castle for seven years, and I've been recommended for the post of housekeeper when Mrs. Fairfax takes her leave at the end of the year. Should you require assistance, I should be happy to fetch Mrs. Fairfax for you." She turned, giving the duke her back and her dismissal, but she only made it a few steps when the duke spoke again, rendering her legs useless.

"I saw my dear brother sneak you back into the castle this morning. Tell me, Jones, is your character always so morally questionable? Perhaps Her Grace should be made aware of your immorality before she gives you further consideration for the post of housekeeper."

Her Grace was very well aware of her relationship with Stephen and had even encouraged it, giving Ethel more afternoons off than were appropriate so she could spend time with Stephen. It wasn't the threat of this revelation that had her turning about. It was the fact that the duke had been *spying* on Stephen.

"And are you always a Peeping Tom?" she returned.

She had clearly shocked the man because his mouth opened without sound, his eyebrows going up.

"You're insolent too," he muttered. "That's cause for dismissal."

"Then it's a right good thing you're not in a position to dismiss me. Now then, I should like an answer to my question. Why were you snooping?" She swept her hand around them to indicate the castle and everything it included. "This is my duchess's home, and I'll not allow anyone—even a duke—to go about poking his nose where it doesn't belong."

A door along the corridor opened, making a soft sound as it traveled across the carpet. Ethel didn't move to look though, and she needn't have because the duchess herself stepped forward into Ethel's line of vision.

"Norfolk," she said in her crisp, clear voice. "Is there something you were looking for this morning which you were unable to find? I thought my husband gave you a thorough tour of the *public* spaces of our home yesterday."

The duchess held a quill in her hand, and Ethel thought the woman must have been conducting her usual semiannual inventories about the house with her various ledgers. She must have been in one of the sitting rooms on this floor when she'd overheard them.

The duke's smile was slow and thick with charm. "I do apologize, Your Grace. I became disoriented on my usual morning walk. You know how good exercise is for a person." He gestured to Ethel. "I just happened to come upon Jones here and Mr. Marley."

The duchess crossed her arms over her chest, careful to keep the quill away from her gown as she addressed Norfolk.

"Mr. Marley and Miss Jones's relationship is none of your concern."

Again, the duke raised his eyebrows. "Then you're aware of it? How forward. I didn't realize Dinsmore was home to such a progressive title. A lady's maid and a duke. That's quite a scandal."

Norfolk's words stumbled about in Ethel's mind, interrupted by the sound of the door to the servants' staircase opening and the Duke of Greyfair's voice saying something about being just a moment while he fetched a new coat, but Ethel couldn't have said what exactly was happening around her because Norfolk's words were ricocheting in her head, the noise they made drowning out everything else.

Thankfully the duchess was not so rattled, and she asked, "A lady's maid and a duke?" She gave a soft laugh. "Hardly. Stephen Marley is my husband's distant cousin on his father's side. He's the estate's orchardist."

Norfolk's laugh was not as soft or congenial. "Is that what my brother has led you to believe?" His eyes focused in on Ethel until she thought she might squirm under his gaze. "Is that how Stephen managed to get you into his bed? By convincing you he was as low as you?"

"Norfolk." Greyfair had reached them, and his voice was not kind. He stepped between Ethel and the duchess and stopped in front of Norfolk. "You are a guest in my house, and I will not stand for such language. I demand you leave. Immediately."

Greyfair hadn't been alone, but Ethel couldn't turn. Not now. She knew that scent of apples and ocean air, and she couldn't move.

Duke?

What was Norfolk saying?

Norfolk kept his gaze on her, ignoring Greyfair. "I just

think it is Miss Jones's right to know the truth. Didn't my dear brother tell you?"

Her heart thudded in her chest, bruising her ribs and crushing her hope.

Norfolk's smile was purely evil now with self-satisfaction. "Stephen was born first. He really is the true Duke of Norfolk." Norfolk held out his hands palm up in an act of pure innocence. "I'm only here to right a wrong against my dear brother, perpetrated so many years ago."

Now she did turn. She spun about so quickly Stephen was forced to take a step back.

"Tell me he's lying." She hated the way her voice shook, the way her hands curled into her skirts as if she were forced to hang on to herself to keep from floating away. "Tell me you're not the Duke of Norfolk."

Stephen's eyes were bright with hope, but with each word she spoke, his expression dimmed until it closed entirely.

"No," she whispered, her head shaking without her telling it to do so. "No," she said again, the only thing she could think to do to make it all not true.

To make the man she loved not a duke. To make him Stephen again. Her Stephen. Not a man so far out of her reach as to be denied her entirely.

"I thought I was being generous by asking my brother if he should like his rightful place, but I'm disheartened to find he refused me," Norfolk said, his voice sickly sweet as if his presence here was not laced with ill intent. "I am left with no choice but to demand he take his rightful place as duke. After all, it is his title. I will not be found a liar because of circumstances that were beyond my control." Norfolk shook his head, his frown heavy with exaggerated sadness. "I'm sorry to be the one to tell you this, Miss Jones. But a lady's maid is simply not allowed to marry a duke. Especially not Norfolk. The queen won't allow it."

Ethel wasn't listening though. There was nothing else that needed to be said, and Norfolk's words were superfluous. A lady's maid could not marry a duke. It was simply understood.

Ethel couldn't marry Stephen, the man she loved, because he wasn't the man she had thought him to be.

"Ethel—" Stephen began but she shook her head.

Words wouldn't help now. Too many unfavorable facts had been planted between them.

So for the second time in as many days, she fled.

CHAPTER 6

*E*thel spent a sleepless night in the dungeon.

It sounded far worse than it actually was. She finished her duties for the day, speaking only when necessary before retreating to her sacred space with a wool blanket and a candle. The floor was cold and hard, but sleep wasn't to come anyway.

The sounds of the ocean and her castle settling around her were comforting enough, and she watched as the small square of light so high in the stone wall changed from inky black to muted grays to the first spark of light.

She didn't wait for the sun to come up. She couldn't bear it.

She'd never be able to forget what it had been like to see her castle bathed in sunrise. She wouldn't mourn it though. She would never mourn something so beautiful as what she and Stephen had shared. But the love she held for him would always be tinged with a little sadness.

How much time had she wasted doubting her confidence? Her own worth? And now it was all taken from her.

She washed and dressed before going to the kitchen for

breakfast with the rest of the servants. Mrs. Fairfax would give them the dispatch for the day. She wondered if they were still a household with a guest or if Norfolk had departed as Greyfair commanded. Ethel wasn't sure exactly quite how dukedoms worked, but she feared Norfolk, as cousin to the queen, was more powerful than Greyfair. She could only hope he wasn't as brave.

Perhaps the castle's ghosts had scared him off in the night. Wouldn't that have been grand?

When she reached the kitchen, Mrs. Fairfax was already in her place at the head of the long wooden table where the servants took their meals. She shuffled several papers before her, and Ethel knew contained the day's menus, any lists for the market, and tasks needing to be completed that day which might be out of the ordinary.

Seeing the woman sitting there now Ethel felt a spark of hope that she may one day sit in her place. She stopped, her shoes squeaking against the stone floor as reality settled around her.

She *could* be the housekeeper.

While she'd known all along she had the heart and the passion for it, she hadn't quite understood she had the mechanics for it. She knew precisely what Mrs. Fairfax was reviewing just then and what her day would look like. After breaking her fast and delivering the daily dispatch, she would meet with Cook to discuss the day's menus and then it would be on to the downstairs staff, particularly the scullery maids. They had recently hired several new ones who were proving quite green in their training and had required extra handling by Mrs. Fairfax.

Then it would be on to her morning meeting with Her Grace in which any necessities would be added to the day's agenda and from there Mrs. Fairfax would meet with the requisite staff members to see Her Grace's wishes carried out. And then—

Ethel stopped the runaway train of her thoughts by plunking down on the bench alongside the wooden table. Mrs. Fairfax eyed her over the papers she held in her hands, her mouth a small bow of consternation, but she said nothing. Surely she had heard of the previous day's events. The upstairs maids seated across from Ethel had whispered in their porridge when Ethel took her seat, but Mrs. Fairfax said nothing. She merely met Ethel's gaze and looked away.

Ethel ate her porridge.

She headed above stairs to Her Grace's dressing room just as the sun reached the vestibule of the castle, lighting the stained glass window that made up one wall and flooding the space with a rainbow of light. It was one of the few times Ethel used the main staircase in the house. She just liked seeing the castle wake for the day, and as no one in the family were ever about at that hour, she was safe to do so.

By the time she reached Her Grace's dressing room, she had convinced herself it would be a regular day, just like any day at Dinsmore, and she would go about her usual tasks in caring for the duchess.

She had just started to feel more assured when she found Her Grace fully dressed and waiting for Ethel in her dressing room.

Ethel stumbled on the threshold, her hand gripped around the doorknob as she hadn't quite made it into the room before tripping over her own feet at the sight of the duchess already up and dressed.

"Your Grace?" Ethel questioned, her hand still holding on to the doorknob as if it could right the world about her.

The duchess smiled. "Jones. I've been waiting."

The duchess had been pacing. Ethel could tell by the way the woman swung about in the room when Ethel opened the door. She'd clearly been traveling in the opposite direction and had turned at the sound of the door opening.

"I do beg your pardon, Your Grace. I hadn't realized I was late. Did you wish to see me earlier than usual this morning?" Ethel gestured behind her in the direction of the servants' stairs and the kitchen beyond. "Mrs. Fairfax didn't—"

"I'd like you to assume the role of housekeeper upon Mrs. Fairfax's departure, Jones. I hope you're amenable to the change."

Ethel's hand slipped from the doorknob, the muscles in her arm going lax. "I beg your pardon," she said again but now for entirely different reasons.

Her Grace smiled. "You're the obvious choice for the position, Jones, and I shan't wish to waste any more time in interviewing other candidates. We can begin the transition immediately, so everything will be operational by the time Mrs. Fairfax leaves us after the holidays."

Transition?

Operational?

This was all happening too quickly, and—

Ethel sucked in a breath, pressing her hand to her stomach.

And the only person she wanted to tell about it was Stephen.

The duchess seemed to sense Ethel's distress because she nudged her out of the way and shut the door gently behind her.

"Sit down before you fall down, Jones," the duchess commanded in her no-nonsense way.

Ethel sat directly on the bench of the duchess's dressing table. At any other time, she would have been appalled at her actions. To sit in front of her mistress was one thing, but to take the mistress's seat was far too much.

But Ethel wasn't thinking. Or maybe it was she was

thinking too much. Whichever it was it had left her mind void of sense and reason.

The duchess sat beside Ethel on the bench, looping one arm around her shoulders. The duchess had always been demonstrably friendlier than any mistress Ethel had ever witnessed, but this was even a bit much for Her Grace's usual kindness, and Ethel felt the very real threat of tears.

The last thing she wanted right then was kindness. It had taken all of her resolve to pick herself up off the dungeon floor and return to her duties. Her duties were clear cut and routine, and that was exactly what she needed just then. Not kindness.

It was like when Stephen encouraged her to death when clearly she was headed toward disaster.

Stephen.

A single tear leaked from her left eye, and she was grateful it was on the opposite side as the one on which the duchess sat.

"Jones, you have the unfortunate circumstance of knowing my sisters, yes?"

Ethel could only nod, the tears having now taken control of her tongue. The duchess's sisters visited often with their families, even the blustery man affectionately called Uncle Herman and his new wife, a tall woman called only Aunt Emma. On their last visit, they had even brought a puppy with them whom Argus, Greyfair's wolfhound, had deemed a nuisance. The puppy had terrorized poor Argus relentlessly until it left with Uncle Herman and Aunt Emma.

"Do you know why, of the three sisters, I was chosen for the marriage contract with Greyfair?"

The tears stopped as suddenly as they had come on, replaced with an odd sense of curiosity. Ethel could clearly remember the day the duchess had arrived at Dinsmore. She'd nearly died when a storm had washed out the causeway to the castle and sent the carriage the duchess was riding in into the sea.

"I'm afraid I do not," Ethel managed.

"I was chosen because my older sister is beautiful and my younger sister is smart, and I was not anything."

Ethel started at this, pulling away from the duchess to stare at her incredulously. "Your Grace," she said sharply, but the duchess held up a hand.

"It's the truth," the duchess said with a shrug. "I was the middle sister, and I had nothing to commend me. Adaline had her beauty, and questionable as it might have been, Alice had her intellect." The duchess had a wry smile on her face as she spoke of her younger sister, and Ethel wondered what the story was behind that, but the duchess went on. "Everyone knew Adaline and Alice had other reasons to win a husband, but I had nothing. I simply wasn't good enough."

Ethel pushed to her feet and turned on the duchess. "Your Grace, I won't sit here and listen to you disparage yourself. Dinsmore is a better place since you've arrived, and the people in it wouldn't be who we are today without you. You simply can't speak ill of yourself. I won't allow it." As soon as the last word left her lips, Ethel registered the knowing grin on the duchess's lips. "Oh," Ethel said quietly. "This isn't about you, is it?"

The duchess stood, her grin melting into a smile. "You know perfectly well it's not. Do you see how quickly you defended me when I said I wasn't good enough? Why did you not have the same reaction when Norfolk said you weren't good enough for Stephen?"

Ethel's eyes widened. "Because that's different, Your Grace. I'm a lady's maid, and Stephen's a duke."

"You're a housekeeper, and Stephen's an orchardist. You're a friend, and Stephen is a cousin. You're a woman, and Stephen is a man." The duchess paused in her recitation as

Ethel felt something growing inside of her, pushing out the despair she'd felt for the past eighteen hours. "I can keep applying labels, Jones, or you can see it for what it is. Two people who love each other and who have the possibility of creating a beautiful future." The duchess stepped forward and took Ethel's shoulders into her hands. "There is no such thing as good enough, Jones. It's a simple matter of finding where you're meant to be. It's only a question of whether or not you love him and if he loves you. The rest means little."

Ethel shook her head, feeling the sting of tears once more. "But that isn't true, Your Grace. Stephen's station is—"

"As the cousin to the Duke of Greyfair and the orchardist at Dinsmore Castle. A perfectly respectable match for the castle's housekeeper." The duchess shook her head. "Stephen isn't suddenly a duke because one man says he is."

"But he was born—"

"We all were born, Jones, and none of us had a say in it. We only get to decide who we become, and from what I've seen, Stephen has chosen to be your husband. How many times did he propose before you agreed to marry him? It seems heartless to repay such tenacity by running away so easily."

It was the closest thing to an accusation the duchess had ever made, and the worst part of it was, it was deserved. Ethel had run away. Twice. As soon as she had faced a reminder of her greatest fear—that she wasn't good enough for Stephen—she'd fled. She'd fled from the chaos of it, from the unknown, from the impossibility of loving someone as amazing as Stephen. At the possibility of never being enough for whatever might come along.

She'd never even given herself a chance.

The duchess released her. "Jones, tell me this. When you're with Stephen, is your time marked by silence or words?" Ethel frowned, puzzled at the question, and the duchess went on. "Words are meant to take you from one point to another, but if you're already where you're meant to be words are unnecessary."

Unbidden, the night in their cottage came back to her, and Ethel could feel the blood rush through her veins at the memory. Sitting there, holding each other's hand in complete silence, only the sound of their hearts beating, the fire crackling, and the night air moving outside to fill the space around them.

It was always like that between them, an easiness that didn't require words, a rightness that just was.

The duchess glanced back at the clock on her dressing table. "Norfolk told my husband he intends to leave first thing this morning." She looked back at Ethel, that knowing grin back on her face. "Perhaps there's something else you'd like to say to him before he goes."

* * *

STEPHEN WAITED IN THE VESTIBULE.

He used a cane today, not wanting the bulk of his crutch to slow him down that morning. He had dressed for the occasion, exchanging his usual wool coat and trousers for an ensemble that held no repaired patches or ungainly seams where he'd tried to fix it himself. He'd even tamed his hair instead of sticking his felt hat atop his head.

Somewhere down the corridor the grandfather clock ticked, and the distant sound of breakfast being laid could be heard in the far reaches of the castle. Lucas said Norfolk planned to leave at first light, and Stephen planned to be there to see him off.

Standing in the corridor yesterday, watching the love of his life run away from him, Stephen realized something very important.

Who his birth family was mattered nothing to him so long as he was nothing like them. Witnessing his twin brother's malicious behavior the previous day had righted things that had been at odds in his mind since he was a little boy, and any questions he might have left held no meaning to him. Because he knew one thing.

He was a better man for having been discarded.

It was no surprise when footfalls sounded on the stairs above him. He straightened his cuff and lapels and adjusted his grip on his cane. When Norfolk came around the last landing of the double revolution staircase, Stephen was startled to see his brother also carrying a cane. It was a moment before he realized the man carried it as an accessory and not to aid his mobility, but the sight of the man carrying the very thing on which Stephen rested was disconcerting.

"Norfolk," Stephen said before the man could utter a greeting. "I have something to say before you leave."

The duke descended the stairs slowly, taking each step with great care, and Stephen couldn't shake the feeling the man was doing it deliberately, to show off his ease of movement. After an interminable time, Norfolk stepped off the stair and stopped in front of Stephen.

"What is it, brother? I must say I've already been disappointed enough by this meeting. I had hoped not to resort to such low brow tactics to make you see the way things must be."

Stephen opened his mouth to tell Norfolk exactly how things would be. Stephen would submit to whatever machinations his twin brother sought, but the man was to leave Ethel Jones alone. Forever. But Stephen was stopped by the sound of a soft step behind him. He turned only his head to find Lucas standing in the shadows of the staircase, his arms crossed over his chest, his gaze level and steady on Norfolk.

He didn't speak, but then Stephen knew that wasn't why his cousin was there.

His cousin always stood behind him.

For a moment he was back on the ridge yesterday morning, and he wondered once again at the strange look his cousin had worn for a flash that Stephen still hadn't interpreted.

He turned back to Norfolk though, and once again opened his mouth to—

Stampede.

He looked up at the sound of riotous footfalls on the stairs, the sound of muffled voices, and then Ethel Jones, flying around the landing of the staircase, her hand raised, a single finger pointed in condemnation at the Duke of Norfolk.

"Oi!" she yelled from the top of the stairs. "You." She all but seethed the single word.

She was not sedate in her journey down the stairs as Norfolk had been. In fact, Stephen was slightly scared she'd fall down most of them in her rush to get to the bottom when she did the strangest thing of all.

She stepped in front of him, standing between Stephen and Norfolk, all five foot two inches of her. Stephen towered above her, but she might as well have been a Viking warrior for the power she exuded.

"Listen here, Norfolk. It's time for you to bugger off and leave us alone." She flung her hand behind her, plowing it directly into Stephen's chest so he was forced to take a step back. "This one's mine."

Never in his life had Stephen heard anything more wonderful nor as frightening. He looked at Norfolk who appeared as though he were being attacked by a tree frog. Footsteps on the stairs behind him had Stephen glancing back to find Amelia descending the steps until she stood next to her husband, an obviously blank expression on her features.

He turned back to his avenging Viking warrior.

His avenging Viking warrior.

"I might be the daughter of a fisherman and a seamstress, but I've worked hard for everything I've got, and that makes me a damn sight better than anything you lay claim to." She stuck a thumb into her own chest. "I've made something of myself from nothing, and if you think you can scare me off with your fancy meaningless titles, let me tell you one thing."

Heaven above if she didn't take a step forward, pushing herself right under Norfolk's nose until he was forced to bend his neck unnaturally or fall out the front door in order to see her.

"Yer goin' to 'ave to do better 'an that, gov," she whispered, her voice thick with the accent of the village and the harbor beyond.

Norfolk's face screwed up as though he had just stepped in a horse plop.

Stephen bit his lip to keep the laugh from escaping when he realized suddenly they weren't alone. Mrs. Fairfax had appeared in the corridor beyond that led to the library and behind her were a flank of maids all carrying brooms. The stairs were lined with footmen carrying coal pails and rubbish bins. Even Cook stood in the shadow of the staircase, a meat cleaver in one hand.

Hell's teeth, the staff had arrived, and they were armed.

He wanted to believe they were there for him, but he knew better as his gaze landed on the woman before him.

The Duke of Norfolk was quite simply outnumbered, and the fiercest of them all was their lady general.

Stephen swung his gaze back to his brother as a curt knock at the door cut through the tension like a blade.

Lucas stepped away from the stair. "Ah, excellent timing.

Norfolk, old man, would you mind opening the door and letting our guest in?"

Norfolk's expression did not improve. He eyed the doorknob as though it might bite him.

"I beg your pardon, Greyfair." His accent was suddenly crisper than normal.

"Open the door. Don't leave our guest standing out there."

Norfolk looked to Ethel. "Have her do it. She's the maid."

"Lady's maid," Lucas corrected. "Lady's maids don't open doors. Don't be ridiculous, Norfolk," he said with a laugh. "Go on. Open the door."

Norfolk took a step back and to the side, his hand closing around the doorknob only after eyeing it speculatively.

The door groaned open, the weight of the oak straining on the hinges. As nothing had gone as imagined that morning, Stephen couldn't begin to fathom who might be on the other side, and who did appear was—

A complete stranger.

"Bartleby," Lucas greeted the man on the other side of the door. "You made it."

Bartleby was a smallish man wearing a felt bowler Derby hat with a pheasant feather stuck along one side and round dark spectacles that were nearly lost in his overgrown beard of red and brown fuzz. He wore a suit that originated on Bond Street and had likely been neatly pressed at one point but now resembled a feed bag.

"Your Grace." Mr. Bartleby came forward with a neat bow. "My train derailed at King's Lynn, I'm afraid. I came the rest of the way by horse cart. I know how imperative it was that you receive these documents." He reached into the leather satchel he carried at his side and extended a sheaf of crisply folded papers to Lucas.

Lucas accepted them, saying, "And is everything as I thought it might be?"

Bartleby closed his satchel, tucking the leather strap back through the clasp. "Precisely, Your Grace. Everything is how it should be."

Lucas took a moment to unfold the papers, his eyes scanning rapidly across the page as he continued. "Norfolk, this is one of my solicitors, the Honorable William Bartleby. His brother is the Earl of Chelmsford. You might be familiar with the family."

Norfolk stood uncomfortably against the now-closed door and eyed the little man with an almost imperceptible nod. "Good day," he managed.

Bartleby only nodded in return, not bothering with a bow as would have been called upon by Norfolk's title. He looked back to Greyfair, his expression expectant.

Lucas shuffled the papers back together and looked up. "I wrote Bartleby as soon as I received your letter, Norfolk. I thought you might be coming here to question matters, and it appears I was right. I had Bartleby pull the birth registrations which named the Duke and the Duchess of Norfolk as parents. Should you like to see them?"

Norfolk straightened away from the door, his gaze wary. "Birth registrations?"

Lucas nodded. "As you're well aware, birth registrations were required at the time you were born. Your parents would have been called upon to register your birth with the local registrar." Lucas handed Norfolk one of the pieces of paper.

Stephen held his breath, his eyes fixated on the sheet of paper.

"Cheese and crust," Ethel whispered beside him, and reflexively, he reached out, drawing her back against him, his hand on her shoulder as Norfolk took the paper and examined it.

Confusion knit his brow as he looked up. "This is only the

registration of my birth. Where's the registration for Stephen?"

Lucas lifted both eyebrows in mock exaggeration. "Who?"

Norfolk's expression turned furious. "Do not play games with me, Greyfair." He shook the paper at Lucas. "Where is Stephen's birth registration?"

"Ah, you mean my cousin, Stephen Marley?" Lucas asked in clarification.

Stephen's gaze moved between the two men in some sort of twisted match of wits.

"I mean Stephen Laurie, the Duke of Norfolk."

Bartleby pushed up his spectacles. "You're the Duke of Norfolk, Your Grace. Are you sure you're well?"

"I don't know about this Stephen Laurie you speak of, but I have a copy of the birth registration from my cousin, Stephen Marley." Here Lucas handed Norfolk the second sheet of paper.

Norfolk snatched it, nearly ripping the page in his haste. He scanned the document, once, twice, thrice. When he looked up, he shook the paper in his anger. "This is a lie. Stephen Marley doesn't exist."

"But you just said he was the Duke of Norfolk," Bartleby reasoned. "Which is it?"

Norfolk's mouth opened and closed twice without sound before his eyes dropped back to the paper he still held in his hand, Stephen's birth registration. Stephen let go of Ethel, squeezing her shoulder before stepping around her to take his own birth registration from Norfolk. The man was either too irate or too dazed to put up a fight and let the paper slip from his hand.

Stephen studied the paper, trying to make sense of what it said.

The document listed a mother and father he'd never heard of, and there in neat black letters was his own name.

He looked up to find his cousin watching him carefully. Stephen didn't know what game his cousin played, so he remained silent, holding on to a piece of paper that either told a lie or spoke the truth.

Lucas walked around their little group then and opened the mammoth oak door. The sound of birdsong and ocean filtered in along with the distant chatter of the stable hands. It was just another morning at Dinsmore Castle, and yet everything was different.

Stephen watched Lucas, registering the press of Ethel against his shoulder at the same time.

"Norfolk, should you decide to go to Her Majesty the Queen with your story, I should only ask one thing of you." Lucas paused here, clearly waiting for Norfolk to meet his gaze. When the man finally looked up from his own birth registration, his face was a mask of confusion and anger. Lucas's smile grew as he spoke. "I only ask that I be allowed to attend your audience. I'd very much like to witness the queen's reaction when you tell her the rightful Duke of Norfolk is a man who doesn't exist."

Norfolk moved to the door in a haze, his lips parted, but his expression clouded. Bartleby stepped forward and snatched the remaining paper from his grasp.

"That's property of Bartleby and Jacobs," he intoned imperiously.

Norfolk sneered and glanced behind him. He met Stephen's gaze but didn't speak, and with that he simply walked out of Dinsmore Castle.

Lucas pulled the door shut behind him, letting the wooden beam that locked it fall into place with a satisfying clunk.

Mrs. Fairfax clapped her hands efficiently. "That's it then," she called. "Our guest has departed. The rooms must be set to rights. Come with me," she said, gesturing to the maids behind her, and in a blink, the battalion of servants returned to their duties as though nothing at all had occurred in the castle vestibule.

Stephen continued to stare at his cousin as he straightened from the door, ensuring it was properly locked. Vaguely the muffled sound of departing hoof falls could be heard, but no voices carried over the sound.

Stephen held up his birth registration. "What is this?"

"It's your birth registration," Lucas pointed out the obvious.

Stephen only frowned.

Lucas sighed and crossed his arms back over his chest. "You tell me you don't know where you've come from, Stephen Marley, and yet the person who knows exactly where you've been has stood next to you for twenty-eight years, and you've never asked him once who you are." Lucas reached out and tapped the paper in Stephen's hand. "This is who you are."

Stephen wanted to look back down at the paper, but he couldn't pry his eyes from his cousin, this man who had grown up with him, had stood next to him, had stood *with* him. How could Stephen have been so blind?

Lucas shook his head now. "Did you ever wonder why I was an only child? My mother lost three babies in her life. One before me and two after me. She cried, Stephen. She cried so terribly much, and I remember being a little boy and helpless to stop her tears. And then you came.

"There was a rainstorm, a bad one, and my parents were agitated. I could tell as much by the way my father paced, and my mother kept checking the windows. They were waiting for something, and I soon realized they were waiting for you. You arrived at Lagameer Hall crying your bloody head off. You were swaddled in a blanket with pink roses stitched along its edges. For the first three days after your arrival, I thought you were a girl." Lucas nodded at the paper. "Your birth had to be registered, and my father didn't want the oversight drawing unwanted attention, so my mother chose your name, and my father devised a plausible story to explain away your presence." Here Lucas leaned forward, pointing out the names that filled the spaces for the identities of the mother and father of Stephen Marley. "Arthur and Arlene Marley were your mother's cousins. They had recently died in a carriage accident. There was no one to prove one way or the other that they had had a child, so my father made them your parents." Lucas moved his finger to the line where Stephen's name had been filled in. "My mother chose Stephen for Saint Stephen." Lucas straightened, crossing his arms again. "Apparently you kept pushing at your twisted foot as if you would straighten it through sheer will. She said anyone with tenacity like that would be a builder of great things." Lucas shook his head. "I don't know how she could think that. You were afraid of carrots."

Emotion had been rising inside of him, but at this, Stephen started. "Carrots?"

"Mmm," Lucas murmured. "Scared to death of them. I made up a song and dance to get you to eat them."

"Do it." Stephen spoke the words before he realized he would, and Lucas's eyes widened in horror.

"Absolutely not."

Quietly Amelia stepped up to their group and cleared her throat, pretending not to watch while clearly watching.

"Do it for me," Stephen said, holding a hand to his chest. "I'm a poor relation from a troubled beginning."

Lucas's expression was fierce as he glared at Stephen. "You're heartless."

"I'm a broken man," Stephen returned.

Lucas cast a woeful glance in his wife's direction before clearing his throat. He began to move, pumping his arms up and down like a marionette and turning about in a circle. "Carrots, carrots, from the ground," he began in a singsong voice. "Carrots, carrots, nice and round. Carrots that you should eat. Because carrots are good for your feet." This was apparently the end of the song because Lucas finished with a little salute and bow.

"Dear God, I think I'm cured," Stephen whispered at the same time Ethel hid a snort of laughter behind her hand, and Amelia stared.

Lucas's frowned rivaled any of the frowns he'd ever given previously, and Lucas was superb at frowning.

But that didn't matter. Lucas knew him—knew *him*—and somehow Stephen had never thought to ask but then—

"Why did you never tell me any of this?" Stephen couldn't make his voice any louder.

"Because you never asked," Lucas said. "I never knew you felt your family was somewhere else, that they had abandoned you." He spread his arms, his smile almost goofy. "We've been here this whole time, you dunderhead."

Stephen dropped his crutch as he stepped into his cousin's arms and hugged the bastard until he thought his organs might pop from his body. And he continued hugging him until Amelia called out, "Are you two finished with this exploration of emotion?" He backed away far enough to look at her. She'd slung an arm around Ethel who had tears streaming down her cheeks. Amelia though was smiling as she said, "We've a wedding to plan."

CHAPTER 7

*E*veryone came to their wedding.
Everyone.

Uncle Herman and Aunt Emma brought them—much to Argus's consternation—a puppy. It was some kind of collie and thankfully did not possess the menacing streak the previous puppy had. Ava promptly named the dog Aurelia. Ethel thought this quite a mouthful for such a small creature, but Ava was adamant, so the name stuck, and by the end of the day, Argus had taken to guarding Aurelia while she napped. It was a match that was already proving it was meant to last.

Ethel Jones married Stephen Marley in the little stone chapel of her beloved castle on a warm autumn day, the air thick with the smell of harvested apples.

Ethel's mother came all the way from France, sporting—of all things—a tan from her trip to Italy with her sister. She wasn't staying long though. She must return to France before the start of the autumnal markets. She had her eye on a trip to Greece this time.

The duchess had insisted on decorating the chapel with

hothouse roses shipped in from London. The blooms of yellow and red and white brought the warmth of autumn into the stone space and complimented the ribbon sashes the girls had made for each pew.

But loveliest of all was the surprise trip to London Her Grace had arranged for Ethel to find a wedding gown. Ethel had insisted it wasn't necessary, but Her Grace explained to Ethel that a trip to London was always necessary. Even Mrs. Fairfax agreed and joined them for the journey. There they met Her Grace's sisters and visited a place called Marlborough Street where Ethel spent luxurious hours in a modiste shop sipping fragrant tea, stuffing herself with cream buns, and being generally doted on and pampered. It had been exquisite.

But seeing Stephen's eyes light up when he saw her gown of cream silk with its rows of careful beading down the bodice that made her look and feel like a waterfall come to life was better than any trip to London, no matter how decadent the buns.

The chapel was anything but quiet as they exchanged their vows. Lord and Lady Aylesford's son, Lucas, had just started talking and being in such proximity to his namesake had him babbling incessantly while Ava and Annie cooed over their baby daughter, Lydia. The girls would later discuss their disappointment in names that started with the letter *L*. Lady Knighton and her husband sat on the side of the chapel so there was ample light by which their daughter, Emma, could read while baby Ashfield slept in his father's arms.

Mrs. Fairfax and Cook stood at the back, dabbing at their eyes with handkerchiefs. What seats weren't filled with family were taken up by the maids and footmen who had so ardently defended the castle's lady's maid and who would soon follow her as their housekeeper.

Ethel swore her love to a man who might have been born

a duke but had become a beloved cousin, a dear friend, and finally her husband.

Ethel smiled through the whole of it, at the buzzing that surrounded them, the evidence of all of the people who loved them and wished to be there for them.

Their wedding breakfast was held in the orchard. The sun warmed their shoulders, and the air was perfumed with the salt of the ocean and the tang of the harvest. Tables had been set up and laden with a feast that would please a king, the feature of which was Mrs. Fairfax's apple butter. They ate and drank and laughed, and Ethel smiled, thinking how impossible it all was.

As the sun reached its highest peak, the fiddlers from the village began to play. Dancing was contagious, and soon Ethel found herself passed from gentleman to gentleman right down to little Ash himself. Stephen found himself accosted by each of the Atwood sisters and even Aunt Emma.

Much later, when all the festivities were finished, they sat on their bed in their cottage amongst the apple trees. Sat because then they could watch the last of the dying sun as it washed over Dinsmore Castle through the windows that lined the opposite wall. They sat shoulder to shoulder, she still in her cream silk wedding gown, he in his suit, tie still knotted perfectly as Uncle Herman had done earlier that day. This time Stephen had taken her hand into his, and he cradled it in his lap.

"Husband," she ventured, not wishing to break the silence that blanketed them. "I know this might sound heartless, but I'm very glad your family discarded you." She turned her head to meet his gaze as she said, "If they hadn't, I never would have found you, and you never would have found where you were meant to be."

His smile was slow as he dipped his head to kiss her, softly, tenderly, and forever.

They had heard nary a word from the Duke of Norfolk in the several weeks since he'd departed Dinsmore in such a state. Rumors in London were he had escaped to America on a freighter out of Liverpool under an assumed name. The queen was livid.

After some time, Ethel looked up at her husband. "Do you regret it? Not accepting Norfolk's offer?"

"To be a duke?" Stephen asked, his gaze steady on the view outside their cottage's windows. "Why would I?"

She followed his gaze, taking in the rambling orchards and her castle, the very foundation on which they would build their lives.

She shrugged as best her position would allow it. "To be a duke is a mighty thing."

Finally he looked at her, his expression serious. "To be your husband is even better," he said and kissed her.

They watched the sun set on Dinsmore, the color washing over the castle until it was swept out to sea. They watched it and said nothing at all.

ABOUT THE AUTHOR

Jessie decided to be a writer because there were too many lives she wanted to live to just pick one.

Taking her history degree dangerously, Jessie tells the stories of courageous heroines, the men who dared to love them, and the world that tried to defeat them.

Jessie makes her home in New Hampshire where she lives with her husband and two very opinionated Basset hounds. For more, visit her website at jessieclever.com.

Made in United States
Cleveland, OH
23 January 2025